CHOICE STORIES
for
CHILDREN

CHOICE STORIES
for
CHILDREN

Selected by
ERNEST LLOYD

Illustrated by Frank McMillan

Reprinted by:

ANGELA'S BOOK SHELF

9746 N. MASON ROAD
WHEELER, MICHIGAN 48662
(Mail order only)

Choice Stories is a selection of stories from four out of print books

- Scrapbook stories
- Lost Jewels
- Golden Grains vol. I
- Golden Grains vol. III

Contents

GRUMBLING TOMMY

THE fire blazed brightly, and everything looked comfortable in the nice, cozy room. Tommy sat by the fire, still holding, the book he had been reading. His mother was sitting at the table, at her work. The old tabby cat purred away in front of the fender, the kettle was singing on the hob, and the old clock ticking away-in the corner. What a picture of warmth and comfort it was!

Outside all was very different. It had been snowing nearly the whole day, but the snow had turned into sleet and rain, which kept beating at the windows as though it wanted to get inside. As Tommy listened to it, he thought how cold it must be outside. This thought led to another, which he soon put into words.

" -Mother," he said, " when shall I have my new overcoat? You know you promised me I should have one this winter."

There was a look of trouble on his mother's face as she replied,--

" I am afraid, Tommy dear, I shall not be able to get you a new coat this winter -certainly not at present. I am very, very sorry. I did hope to do so, but you know things have not turned out as I ex-pected, and-"

Tommy interrupted her with a burst of impatience:-

"I never have anything like other boys! "

"Tommy! Tommy!" said his mother, in a gentle, half-reproving tone, "you know you have all that a kind mother can possibly get for you, and you know how delighted I should be for you to have a new coat if I could possibly afford one, but I see no chance of it at present."

" I wonder why God lets us be so poor?" exclaimed Tommy, in the same fretful way" Look at cousin Robbie, and Willie

Thompson, and---and---"

" And what? " asked his mother.

" They always get new coats when they want them," pouted Tommy.

" If they do, I am sure they ought to be very thankful," said his mother. " But think, Tommy, of the many in the streets who, in this bitter weather, have scarcely any clothes to cover them, and scarcely any food to eat; poor boys who have no home to shelter them, but who will have to pass the night upon some cold stone step, or in some empty cart. Think of them, Tommy, and thank God that you, have a comfortable home, with plenty to eat and drink, and clothes which are nice and warm, if they are not very fine. Besides," she added cheerfully, "I am going to get to work upon your old coat tomorrow, and put some new buttons on it, and new binding, and I shall brighten it up so, and make it look so much like a new one, that you will hardly know it again. There, give me a kiss, and go to bed; you are tired and out of sorts."

Tommy was very much out of sorts. He gave his mother a forced kiss, and went grumbling to bed.

His mother was very sad. She had had a hard struggle since their father died, to keep Tommy and his little sister Lucy in comfort. She had worked cheerfully and lovingly, and never murmured at her poverty. But Tommy's grumbling grieved and distressed her, and her tears fell upon her work as she thought how hard it was to be poor.

Soon after Tommy went to bed he fell asleep. But he roused again by-and-by. He heard his mother locking the doors below, and coming up stairs. She entered his room, tucked the bedclothes up comfortably, and kissed him. Tommy half opened his sleepy eyes, and said, Good-night, mother." He heard her go out, and open and shut her own door. He wondered whether he had distressed her much by his grumbling, and thought he had, and felt uneasy and troubled about it. He listened to the rain as it pattered against his window, and to the wind moaning in the chimney, and thought of the poor homeless boys his mother spoke of. He heard the old clock down stairs strike one, and the policeman's slow, heavy step pass under his window, and then he dropped off to sleep again. By-and-by he thought he heard his door open. He looked out from under the bedclothes to see what it was. The light from a policeman's lantern dazzled his sleepy eyes, and the policeman himself, tall and looking very severe, stood beside his bed. Tommy was terribly frightened. He would have popped his head under the bedclothes again, but the big policeman's gruff voice stopped him, Little grumbler," he said, "discontented. unthankful boy, get up and come along with me!"

"Where to, sir?" Tommy timidly asked.

"Out into the streets," said the policeman, " to see how it fares with the poor boys who have no warm beds, no comfortable homes, and no kind mother to take care of them."

The thought of turning out of his warm bed into the streets, on such a night, made Tommy shudder.

"But it's so cold," he pleaded.

"I know it is,"said the policeman, bitterly cold. Come along!" Tommy felt that it was of no use trying to resist the stern policeman, and so be crept, shivering, out of bed.

"Put on your things," said the policeman.

Tommy did so.

"Where are your boots?"

"I left them down stairs," replied Tommy, " and the door's locked, and mother's got the key, and we can't get in there."

How glad he was of an excuse for not going out. But the policeman was not to be moved.

"Never mind," be said; "few of the boys in the streets have anything on their feet. You will be no worse off than they are. Come along!"

"But I haven't got my overcoat and comforter, nor my

cap," urged Tommy, 'With a discontented whine.

The policeman looked more severe than ever. "Overcoat! comforter! " he said. "You have a nice warm jacket now. Why! the boys you will see have scarcely a bit of anything to cover them." And with that he laid hold of Tommy's arm, and led him, too frightened to cry out, down the stairs, out of the door, into the street.

How dreadfully cold it was, to be sure! As Tommy stepped out upon the halffrozen snow, he shuddered and shivered from head to foot. The rain and sleet beat about his head and face until his nose and ears tingled again, and his eyes were almost blinded. The wind seemed as though it would freeze his very blood. But the terrible policeman dragged him on through rain, and sleet, and wind, and snow, until they came to a stable-yard where an empty, covered wagon was put up for the night. The policeman turned the light of his lantern into it, and there, crouching and shivering in one corner, was what looked like a bundle of rags, with two or three little naked feet peeping out from underneath, and two thin, pale faces looking out from above.

"Halloo! " said the policeman. " What are you doing here? " A weak little voice replied, " Please, sir, we ain't a doin' no harm to nobody."

"Is that you, Bobby ? " asked the policeman.

"Yes, sir, me and Billy."

" Well," said the policeman, and Tommy noticed that his voice was kinder, and more gentle, " mind you don't make a noise, and you can stay here all night." And the little voice said, " Thankee, sir."

" And take this little chap with you," said the policeman as he lifted Tommy into the wagon, "and keep him here till I come back."

And he turned away and left the yard. How glad Tommy was to creep into the corner with the other boys, away from the cutting wind! His toes and fingers were numbed with the cold. His teeth chattered. His clothes were drip-ping. His hair was soaked and matted; and the cold drops trickled down his neck. Poor Tommy! He could hold up no longer, but giving way to his wretchedness, he burst into a fit of crying.

"What's the matter?" asked Bobby.

"Oh, it's---so---cold," sobbed Tommy. "It's a shame--it's wicked--to---bring me-out of my---warm---bed---on---such, a night---as this! "

"Cold!" said Bobby. "D'yer call this cold? How'd yer like to be a sittin' on a stone step, with nothin' to keep the wind out, and the rain and snow a-fallin' a-top of yer all the time? *That's* cold, but this-this is comfortable to it."

Poor little fellow! he shivered and trembled in spite of his brave words.

"But we can't sleep here often," said Billy, " the p'lice drives us away, 'ceptin' that one as brought you here; he's a good un. he is."

Tommy went on crying, but less and less as he thought of what they said. Presently Bobby spoke again. " P'r'aps you're hungry, little un?" "No, I'm not hungry," said Tommy, " I'm only cold and miserable."

"I wish I was only cold," said Bobby. " I ain't had nothin' to eat since this mornin', and I shouldn't have had nothin' at all, only a little chap agoin' to school, with a slice of bread'n butter in his hand, see me lookin' hungry, I s'pose, and so he give it to me. He was a kind little feller, wasn't he ? "

"I ain't had nothin' but a pennyworth o' soup," said Billy. " A gen'l'man give me a penny for holdin' his horse, and I got some soup. I ain't had nothin' else."

The talk ended here. Tommy had left off crying. He felt ashamed of himself as he heard what these poor boys said. He thought of all his comforts, and of the miserable lives they must lead, to have no better place to sleep in than a wretched wagon, and nothing to eat for a whole day but a slice of bread and butter, or a basin of soup. Bobby and Billy had dropped off to sleep. The wind seemed to blow into the wagon colder and colder as the night went on. But Tommy's discontent and grumbling were over now, and the more cold he felt, the more he pitied his miserable companions. Poor little fellows! How they shivered and moaned in their sleep! Tommy wished he had his old coat to spread over them. "Ah," he thought, "mother was right. It is a warm and comfortable coat, although it's not very fine." And he shed many bitter tears as he remembered his unthankfulness and discontent. "But when the policeman comes," he thought, "I'll ask him to take these poor boys home with us. Mother will give them a good breakfast, I know."

And so he went on, thinking and shivering, shivering and thinking until at last he heard the policeman's footsteps coming up the yard. Presently, the light of the lantern shone into the wagon, and a voice called, —

"Det up, Tommy, it's dettin' so late."

Tommy jumped up, wondering how the policeman's voice could sound like that, and then everything changed. The cold, hard boards of the wagon turned into soft, warm pillows; the light of the policeman's lantern spread out into the light of day and instead of the tall, stern policeman, there was only his little sister Lucy, laughing beside his bed, in his own little room at home. Tommy rubbed his eyes. " Why," he said, " have I been dreaming? Where are Bobby and Billy ?"

Lucy burst out into a merry laugh, and ran down stairs.

Tommy got out of bed, and kneeling down he said his morning prayer, adding at the close of it: " And, 0 Lord, let me never be a little grumbler again, but a cheerful, contented, and thankful boy."

SOME LITTLE FOLKS

THERE are some little folks that we never can
      please;
They fret about trifles, they trouble and tease,
      Full of discontent, even at play ;
Till their friends are worn out, and are heartily glad
When bed-time is come, and each cross lass or lad
      Is quiet and out of the way.

There are some little folks so good tempered and
      sweet
That to see their bright faces is always a treat;
And their friends can quite trust them, they know;
They amuse themselves nicely with some plan or
      play,
Take care not to worry or get in the way,
      And are welcome wherever they go.

Joe Benton's Coals of Fire

IT WAS a lovely morning; the sun was shining brightly, and the air was fragrant with violets and lilacs when Joe Benton sprang out the back door, shouting for joy over the anticipated pleasures of the holiday. "I'll have time to run to the brook before breakfast and see if my boat is all right," he said to himself. "We boys are to meet and launch her at nine o'clock, and the captain ought to be up on time."

So Joe hastened down to the cave where the precious boat was hidden. As he neared the place, an exclamation of surprise escaped him. There were signs of some intruder, and the big stone before the cave had been rolled away. Hastily drawing forth his treasure, he burst into loud cries of dismay; for there was the beautiful little boat which Cousin Herbert had given him, with its gay sails split into many shreds, and a large hole bored in the bottom.

Joe stood for a moment, motionless with grief and surprise; then, with a face as red as a peony, he burst forth: "I know who did it! It was Fritz Brown, and he was angry because I didn't ask him to come to the launching. But I'll pay him back for this," said Joe. Hastily pushing back the ruined boat, he went a little farther down the road. He fastened a piece of string across the footpath a few inches from the ground and carefully hid himself in the bushes.

Presently a step was heard, and Joe eagerly peeped out. How provoking! Instead of Fritz, it was Cousin Herbert, the last person he cared to see. Joe tried to lie very quiet; but it was all in vain. Cousin Herbert's sharp eyes caught a

As soon as Fritz saw Joe, he hurried to present to him a beautiful
flag he had bought for the sailboat with part of his egg money.

curious movement in the bushes, and, brushing them right
and left, he soon came upon Joe. "How's this?" cried he,
looking straight into the boy's face; but Joe answered not a
word. "You're not ashamed to tell me what you were
doing?"

"No, I'm not," said Joe sturdily, after a short pause. "I'll tell you the whole story." Out it tumbled, down to the closing threat. "I mean to make him smart for it," said Joe.

"What do you mean to do?"

"You see, Fritz carries a basket of eggs to the store every morning, and I plan to trip him over this string, and make him smash all of them."

Now Joe knew well enough that he was not showing the right spirit, and he muttered to himself, "Now for a good scolding;" but to his great surprise Cousin Herbert said quietly: "Well, I think Fritz does need some punishment; but this string is an old trick. I can tell you something better than that."

"What?" cried Joe eagerly.

"How would you like to put a few coals of fire on his head?"

"What, and burn him?" said Joe doubtfully.

Cousin Herbert nodded with a queer smile.

Joe clapped his hands. "Now that's just the thing, Cousin Herbert. You see, his hair is so thick he wouldn't get burned much before he'd have time to shake them off; but I'd like to see him jump once. Tell me how to do it, quick!"

" 'If thine enemy be hungry, give him bread to eat; and if he be thirsty, give him water to drink: for thou shalt heap coals of fire upon his head, and the Lord shall reward thee,' " said Cousin Herbert gravely. "I think that's the best kind of punishment Fritz could have."

Joe's face lengthened terribly. "Now, that's no punishment at all."

"Try it once," said Cousin Herbert. "Treat Fritz kindly, and I am certain that he will feel so ashamed and unhappy he would far rather you had given him a severe beating."

Joe was not really a bad boy at heart; but he was now in an ill temper, and he said sullenly: "You said this kind of coals would burn, and they don't at all."

"You're mistaken about that," said his cousin cheerily. "I have known such coals to burn up a great amount of rubbish—malice, envy, ill feeling, revenge, and I don't know how much more—and then leave some cold hearts feeling as warm and pleasant as possible."

Joe drew a long sigh. "Well, tell me a good coal to put on Fritz's head, and I'll see about it."

"You know," said Herbert, smiling, "Fritz is poor and he can seldom buy himself a book, although he loves to read. Now you have quite a library. Suppose—ah, well, I won't suppose anything about it! I'll leave you to find your own coal; but be sure to kindle it with love, for no other fire burns so brightly and so long." With a cheery "good-by," Herbert sprang over the fence and was gone.

Before Joe had time to collect his thoughts, he saw Fritz coming down the lane with a basket of eggs in one hand and a pail of milk in the other.

For one moment, the thought crossed Joe's mind: "What a smash it would have made if Fritz had fallen over the string!" Then he stopped, glad that the string was safe in his pocket.

Fritz looked uncomfortable when he first caught sight of Joe; but the boy began abruptly: "Fritz, have you much time to read now?"

"Sometimes," said Fritz, "when I've driven the cows home, and done all my work; but the trouble is, I've read everything I can get hold of."

"How would you like to take my new book of travels?"

Fritz's eyes danced. "Say, would you let me? I'd be careful with it!"

"Yes," answered Joe, "and perhaps I've some others you'd like to read." Then he added shyly: "Fritz, I would ask you to come and help sail my boat today; but someone has torn up the sails, and made a hole in the bottom. Who do you suppose did it?"

Fritz's head dropped, but after a moment he looked up, and said: "I did it, Joe; but I can't begin to tell you how sorry I am. You did not know I was so mean when you promised me the books."

"Well, I rather thought you did it," said Joe slowly.

"And yet you—" Fritz couldn't get any further. He rushed off without another word.

"That coal does burn. I know Fritz would rather I had smashed every egg in his basket than to have offered him that book." Then Joe went home with a light heart, hungry for his breakfast.

When the captain and the crew of the little vessel met at the appointed hour, they found Fritz there before them trying to repair the damage. As soon as he saw Joe, he hurried to present him with a beautiful little flag he had bought for the boat with part of his egg money that morning. The boat was repaired, and everything turned out as Herbert had said. Joe found that the more he used of this curious kind of coal, the larger supply he had on hand—kind thoughts, kind words, and kind actions.

Joe's playmates, who saw that he was always happy, studied the secret, and when any trouble came up, someone would say: "Let us try a few of Joe Benton's coals." It was astonishing to see how quickly their hearts grew warm toward each other.

Selling a Birthright

"FATHER," said Charley one day, "Mr. Reed is going to take the whole school to Union Hill, where we are to have a dinner and a grand time. We are to choose a captain from the senior class."

"Whom are you going to vote for in the election?"

"Morton, the tallest fellow in school, and the best boy, too, I think. But George has gone over to the opposition."

Father looked at George. "Who is your candidate? Let's hear about it."

"Chester is my choice," said George. "I don't see why he won't make as good a captain as Morton."

"He is not so good a scholar," said Charley. "Besides, he swears sometimes. Then, too, he's buying up votes, and I think that is mean."

George flushed a little, but made no reply.

"George," said his father, "I want you to tell me whether Chester has given you anything to influence your vote."

George hung his head and was slow to reply. There was no escape from his father's question, and at last he answered: "I broke my new bat yesterday playing baseball. Chester gave me his if I would promise to vote for him."

"Did you promise?"

"Yes, father."

"You were wrong, my boy. Your vote is your birthright. Not long ago, when we read how Esau sold his birthright for a mess of pottage, you thought him a foolish man. Now you have sold yours for a secondhand bat. You have sold your influence, as far as it goes, to vote for a boy who, by taking unfair means, shows he is unfit for the position. Now, as you look over the whole affair, do you not think that it is pretty cheap?"

"Yes," answered George; "but I didn't think it was so important."

"If you can be bought with a bat when you are a boy, you may be bought with an office, or with money, when you are a man. I want my sons to be above taking bribes or selling their freedom."

"What should I do?"

"Take the bat back to Chester and tell him how the matter looks to you on further consideration. If he has any honor in him, he will release you from your promise; if he has none, he can hold you to it, and you must keep your word. But take care not to be caught in such a position again."

George wished the old bat were at the bottom of the sea as he carried it back to Chester. He was laughed at, reproached, and held to his promise, as he expected to be; and acquired such a contempt for his candidate's lack of principle that he was glad when he found himself on the losing side the next day. In fact, he joined heartily in the cheers which the winners gave for their friend Morton.

Mattie's Prize

Wnat was Mattie turning over and over in her hand, looking admiringly at it the while? Every now and then a ripple of laughter broke from her lips. She was sitting on the floor in the front room, wishing mother would wake up to hear of her good fortune and help her admire this wonderful prize.

It would not do to awaken her, for she was getting over a long, severe sickness. Mattie, though only eight years old, knew that every hour of sleep was bringing her mother nearer to health again. Still, it was trying for her to sit quietly with such a wonderful thing to tell. She at last decided she could not wait any longer, and she went to find Aunt Fanny.

Aunt Fanny was getting dinner, but she looked up with a smile as Mattie put her rosy face in at the door.

"Is your mother still asleep, Mattie?" she asked.

"Yes. What did Dr. Morris say today?"

"He thinks she will soon be about again. He said it would do her a great deal of good to take a ride, but we must give that up."

"Why, Aunt Fanny?"

"Because we cannot spare the money. You know, dear, your mother's sickness not only keeps her from her students, but it takes many hours from her sewing. We shall have to live very economically for a long time to keep out of debt. So, you see, we cannot spare five dollars for a ride."

"Will it cost that much?"

"I tried my best, and when I had finished, the man said, 'This little girl has fairly earned the prize,' and he put in my hand a five-dollar bill."

"Yes, Mattie. It's no use to go for a little city drive. What your mother needs is a good breath of country or sea air, and it will take a long ride to get that. It is such a lovely afternoon, too," she added regretfully.

"Aunt Fanny, we will go. You get mamma ready, and I will make the arrangements. What time should we start?"

"It is nearly twelve. Say one o'clock," said Aunt Fanny as the little girl rushed off.

It was well for her that the invalid was awake when she returned, for her delightful news certainly would not keep much longer. Her mother was waiting as impatiently as Aunt Fanny for an explanation, and the happy child was eager to give it.

"We were all in school this morning, mother, when Miss Stratton told us that some great man—I did not catch his name—was going around the building to see how our school was managed. After a few minutes he came in with four or five other men. We went through some of the exercises and sang for him.

"Then he said: 'Now I want to hear some of the little girls read aloud. I will give this to the best reader.' And he held up something, I could not see what.

"Miss Stratton called up five girls to read, and I was among them. When it came my turn, mother, I remembered all you had told me about punctuation, distinctness, and expression, and I tried my best. I was the last, and when I finished he said, 'This little girl has fairly earned the prize,' and he put in my hand—see, mamma!"—and Mattie held out her treasure—"a five-dollar bill.

"I danced all the way home and found you asleep. Then I sat down and tried to think of all I could buy for five dollars. I wanted to run right out and get you some oranges and grapes and all sorts of good things. I wanted to buy you a new pair of slippers—yours are so shabby. I wanted to get you—"

"Stop, stop, little daughter! Did you not want to buy something for yourself with your five dollars?"

"Oh, mamma, I have everything I want!"

"I thought I heard a little girl wishing for a new hat and shoes."

"Oh, the old ones will do! Wouldn't I look nice," said Mattie scornfully, "buying myself hats and shoes, when you are sick! Well, I was trying to decide what to buy, and went to ask Aunt Fanny, and she told me about the good a ride would do you. So, mamma, we will go for a ride down to the seashore, and make you well and strong again."

"But, Mattie, it seems too bad to take your prize from you so soon."

"Too bad! As if I cared for the money half as much as I care to get you well! Besides, mother, if you had not taken so much pains to teach me to read well, I would never have had the prize. So, you see, it is really yours, after all. Now let me help Aunt Fanny dress you. Isn't it beautiful to see you have a hat on again!"

It would be quite beyond my power of description to give any idea of that ride. The best part of it, for the little girl, was the sight of a faint flush upon her mother's pale cheeks, a new light in her eyes, a stronger, clearer ring in her weak voice.

After happy, tired Mattie was fast asleep in her own little bed, the mother said: "I was downhearted, Fanny, thinking I must give up the struggle for health; but my little daughter's gift must be repaid by making every effort to get well again. I will get well for her sake."

"Yes, indeed," Aunt Fanny said heartily; "for there are not many little girls who would have no thought of self after winning such a prize."

Annie's Handy Box

"ONE of my glove buttons is gone," said sister Kate, as she was preparing to go out. "How provoking it is! A glove looks so untidy unfastened."

"Wait a minute, sis," said Annie, "I believe I have some glove buttons in my handy box." Opening it, she found a little tin box. She poured the contents in her apron and soon found the required button. Her handy needle and silk quickly sewed it on, and she was well repaid by a kiss from her sister. "Thank you, Annie," said Kate, "your little box of curiosities is a perfect gold mine. You can always find the right thing there." Down the steps she went, quite satisfied that all was right.

"How long have you had that box, Annie?" asked Ned, who was spending a week at the house.

"Ever since she can remember, I guess," said mother, laughing. "She always was careful about little things from the time she could toddle about the floor. She used to make collections of buttons and pretty stones when she was four years old. It is a good habit, though, and I am sure we are all indebted to her every day. It would be a curiosity to keep an account of the calls she has for her handy box."

"I think I will do it," said Ned. "Where can I find a paper and pencil?"

Annie opened her box again and took out the half of an old envelope she had saved, and a piece of pencil someone had swept out of doors.

"You can set down three things to begin with," she

said, laughing—"a glove button, piece of paper, and pencil."

Little Martha came running in holding the string from her cap. She was in "such a hurry."

"Run to Annie," said mother, who was busy making pies.

Up went the box lid, and this time a little bag containing all sorts of odds and ends of old strings and ribbons was inspected. The right thing was there, and, using a threaded needle, Annie sewed it on in a minute's time, and Martha went dancing off to her play.

"No. 4," said Ned, as father came in and asked Annie if she could find a strong piece of string. Another little bag was produced and it contained what was wanted. With a "Thank you, daughter, you are a treasure, and so is your box," he went on his way.

"Take your work and don't stir from that corner today," said Ned; "you'll be wanted. You might set up a store. Well, Tommy, what can we do for you?"

"I have lost my mitten, sister, and I can't make a snow man without it. May I have another?"

"Now, I think you are stuck, Annie," said Ned.

Annie smiled and said to Tommy: "If sister will give you another mitten will you go and look for the lost one?"

The little fellow promised, and was told to go and warm his feet by the fire. Annie took out a paper pattern and a bit of thick cloth, which she quickly cut mitten shape and sewed up, all in fifteen minutes' time.

Ned looked on, dumb with admiration, and secretly resolved to learn a lesson.

Who else would like to have such a handy box? It is useful, not only to yourself, but to others. It will help to form the good habit of saving that which is valuable for use later on.

School Sickness

ONE morning Willie was attacked by a curious but common headache. He had been subject to such attacks before. They seemed worse just before schooltime, decreased rapidly toward noon, and appeared again about one o'clock. As they were growing upon him, mother desired to prevent the attacks in the future.

He was sitting in the big armchair, looking disconsolate, when his mother entered the room. "Come, Willie," said she, "you'll be late to school."

"Oh, mother, I have an awful headache, and I feel sick."

"Indeed! I'm sorry. I'll go and get my castor oil, and then put you to bed."

"Oh, I'm not sick enough to take medicine or go to bed," said Willie, looking a little brighter, but not entirely recovered.

"Well, then, I'll wrap you in my big shawl, and let you sit by the fire. You can study your lesson and recite to me."

"Don't you think it would do me good to run up and see Mr. Winters a little while, mother? I need the fresh air."

He looked longingly out through the open door, where the dog was dozing in the sunshine. The birds were singing, and everything seemed happy outside. But he was an invalid, confined to a warm kitchen. How he did wish he had gone to school! He had not thought his mother would take his plea of sickness so seriously.

"I can't study," he said at last, looking up. "All my books are at school. I didn't know I was going to be at home."

"You needn't worry, if that's all," said the mother. "I remember seeing my books in the attic a few days ago."

"I fear they're too old."

"I don't believe they are much different from the ones you use. I'll go up and look for them."

"Can't I go?" cried Willie eagerly, forgetting his headache.

"No, my dear, you might catch cold. Sit still."

So Willie settled back in his big chair, indeed looking much like an invalid.

While he was alone he could hear in the distance the voices of the children at play during recess. How he longed to be out playing.

When his mother came back with a spelling book, Willie's headache returned. He passed his morning twisting about in the chair and wishing for dinnertime to come. At noon, Johnny, one of his friends, came to see why he had been absent.

"It's nice to be a little sick. I wish I were," said the boy, gazing wistfully at Willie in the big chair.

"No, it's perfectly horrid. I will never be sick again."

"But when are you coming back to school?"

"This afternoon," cried Willie decidedly. "I mean to go to school all my life."

"You must not go to school this afternoon, son. You'll have to wait until you are well," said mother, determined to make a sure cure.

"Oh, mother, can't I go, please? I don't feel sick now."

Johnny, not understanding the situation, looked in amazement at Willie. He wished that his mother would act the same way when he didn't want to go to school.

Willie had a dreary afternoon and was glad when night

came. In the morning he was up bright and early. As soon as his mother appeared, he cried out: "I can go to school to-day, can't I, mother?"

"I'm afr—" began his mother.

Willie broke in: "Now, mother, I just must. I'll go crazy if I have to stay home another day."

"Well, then, you must wear your coat. You mustn't get sick again."

When Willie showed the slightest desire to stay away from school after that, his mother would say: "Willie, don't you feel well? You can stay at home with me today and rest, if you like." But the invitation has never yet been accepted. So far, Willie has carried out his intention not to miss school.

After having learned his lesson, Willie resolutely decided that he would not be absent from school anymore.

Keeper of the Light

MARY'S father was the keeper of a lighthouse on the coast of England. The light of these lamps shines at night to guide ships on their way and to keep them from dangerous rocks and shoals. The lighthouse seems to say: "Take care, sailors, for rocks and sands are here. Keep a good lookout and mind how you sail, or you will be lost."

One afternoon Mary was in the lighthouse alone. Mary's father had trimmed the lamps, and they were ready for lighting when evening came. As he needed to buy some food, he crossed the causeway which led to the land. This causeway was a path over the rocks and sands, which could be used only two or three hours in the day; at other times, the waters rose and covered it. The father intended to hasten home before the tide flowed over this path. Night was coming on, and a storm was rising on the sea. Waves dashed against the rocks, and the wind moaned around the tower.

Mary's mother was dead, and although she was alone, her father had told the girl not to be afraid, for he would soon return. Now there were some rough-looking men behind a rock, who were watching Mary's father. They watched him go to the land.

Who were they? They were "wreckers" who lurked about the coast. If a vessel was driven on the rocks by a storm, they rushed down—not to help the sailors, but to rob them, and to plunder the ship.

The wicked men knew that a little girl was left alone

Mary was alone in the dark lighthouse when the storm broke.

in the lighthouse. They planned to keep her father on the shore all night. Ships filled with rich goods were expected to pass the point before the morning and these men knew if the light did not shine, the vessels would run upon the rocks and be wrecked. How cruel and wicked they were to seek the death of the ships' crews!

Mary's father had filled his basket, and prepared to return to the lighthouse. As he drew near the road leading to the causeway, the wreckers rushed from their hiding place and threw him on the ground. They quickly bound his hands and feet with ropes and carried him into a shed, where he had to lie until morning. It was in vain that he shouted for them to set him free; they only mocked his distress. They then left him in the charge of two men, while they ran back to the shore.

"Oh, Mary, what will you do?" cried the father as he lay in the shed. "There will be no one to light the lamps. Ships may be wrecked, and sailors may be lost."

Mary looked from a narrow window toward the shore, thinking it was time for her father to return. When the clock in the little room struck six, she knew that the water would soon be over the causeway.

An hour passed. The clock struck seven, and Mary still looked toward the beach; but her father was not to be seen. By the time it was eight, the tide was nearly over the causeway; only bits of rock here and there were above the water. "O father, hurry," cried Mary, as though her father could hear her. "Have you forgotten your little girl?" But the only answer was the noise of the waters as they rose higher and higher, and the roar of the wind as it gave notice of the coming storm. Surely there would be no lights that night.

Mary thought of what her mother used to say: "We should pray in every time of need." Quickly she knelt and prayed for help: "O Lord, show me what to do, and bless my father, and bring him home safe."

The water was now over the causeway. The sun had set more than an hour ago, and, as the moon rose, black storm clouds covered it from sight.

The wreckers walked along the shore, looking for some ship to strike on the coast. They hoped that the sailors, not seeing the lights, would think they were far at sea.

At this moment Mary decided she would try to light the lamps. But what could a little girl do? The lamps were far above her reach. She got matches and carried a small stepladder to the spot. After much labor she found that the lamps were still above her head. Then she got a small table and put the stepladder on it. But when she climbed to the top the lights were still beyond her reach. "If I had a stick," she said, "I would tie a match to it, and then I could set a light to the wicks." But no stick was to be found.

The storm was raging with almost hurricane force. The sailors at sea looked along the coast for the light. Where could it be? Had they sailed in the wrong direction? They were lost and knew not which way to steer.

All this time Mary's father was praying that God would take care of his child in the dark and lonely lighthouse.

Mary, frightened and lonely, was about to sit down again, when she thought of the old Bible in the room below. But how could she step on that Book? It was God's Holy Word that her mother had loved to read. "Yet, it is to save life," said she; "and if mother were here, would she not allow me to take it?"

In a minute the large book was brought and placed under the steps, and up she climbed once more. Yes, she was high enough! She touched one wick, then another, and another, until the rays of the lamps shone brightly far above the dark waters.

The father saw the light as he lay in the shed, and thanked God for sending help in the hour of danger. The sailors saw the light, and steered their ships away from the rocks. The wreckers, too, saw the light, and were angry to see that their evil plot had failed.

All that stormy night the lamps cast their rays over the foaming sea; and when the morning came, the father escaped from the shed. Soon he reached the lighthouse and found out how his little girl had stood faithful to duty in the dark hours of storm.

Florie's Birthday Party

FLORIE SWIFT would be eight years old tomorrow, and her mother had promised her the company of six young friends to take dinner with her and spend the afternoon. "You may invite whom you please," mother said.

As soon as lessons were over, the girl went out, accompanied by Ann, the maid, to invite her guests. Ann thought, of course, that Florie would invite Fannie Morris, Jennie Snow, and two or three other close playmates. They lived in large houses on the next street, so Ann started to turn in that direction.

"Where are you going?" asked Florie. "The company I am going to invite don't live there. Those girls have many good times."

On they walked until they came to a narrow street with a none-too-inviting appearance.

"I am going to stop here," said Florie. She opened a rickety door and began to climb the stairs. Stopping at the top of the first flight, she knocked at the door on her right. "Come in," was faintly heard. Florie opened the door and found a girl about her own age sitting in a chair, knitting. This was Mary Gray, the daughter of a woman who had done sewing for Florie's mother. The child was blind, but she held out her hand in the direction of Florie's voice.

"Mrs. Gray," Florie said, "I came to see if you would allow Mary to have dinner with me tomorrow. It is my birthday, and mamma has promised me a little party. I will send for Mary, if you are willing."

(33)

Mrs. Swift greeted blind Mary, Amy, Tommy, and the other guests Florie had invited. It was a delightful party, and everyone had a happy time.

"How good you are, Miss Florie!" the woman replied. "My little child has but few pleasures. I know she will enjoy her visit with you."

"Thank you," said Mary, with a wan smile. "I'll be waiting for the party."

"I will send for you, Mary, at three o'clock tomorrow."

Bidding the mother and daughter good-by, Florie went down the stairs and hurried along to another house near by, where a large boot hung out for a sign. Ann looked at Florie in amazement as she entered this little shop. An old man sat mending shoes, and a little lame boy propped up in a chair was trying to amuse himself with some bits of bright-colored leather.

"Well, Miss Florie," exclaimed the child, "I am so glad you have come! Those roses you sent me a few days ago were so beautiful. I kept them as long as I could."

"I'm glad you liked them, Jamie. I have come to invite you to dinner tomorrow, and you shall have as many roses as you can carry home."

The little fellow glanced at his lame feet, and then at his crutches.

"Never mind, Jamie," the old shoemaker said. "I will carry you to Miss Florie's."

Florie now left for another home on a side street. She stopped at the door of a shabby-looking house, which was occupied by an old woman, formerly a nurse in Florie's family.

"Bless you, Miss Florie, it does me good to see your bright face," said the woman. "No one has been to read the story of the Good Shepherd since you were here, and my old eyes are of little service now."

"Well, nursie, tomorrow will be my birthday, and you are to come to dinner with me. Then I'll read to you if you wish."

"The precious child," said the old woman, "to think of a poor old nurse!"

"Good-by, nursie! I am not through inviting my friends

yet." Beckoning to Ann, Florie walked on a few doors farther and stopped at another home. A weak-looking child not much older than Florie came to the door with a crying baby in her arms.

"Why, Florie," the child exclaimed, "who ever would have thought of seeing you!"

"Where is your mother, Amy?"

"She is washing. The baby is so cross I can't do anything with him. I could not go to church last week because he was not well."

"Do you think your mother will let you come and have dinner with me tomorrow? It's my birthday."

By this time the woman appeared, and Florie asked: "Please, may Amy come to my house tomorrow afternoon? It will be my birthday. We are in the same Sunday school class, and I should like to have her."

"Certainly, miss; I have no objections." The mother and child both seemed happier to have Florie call.

"Where next?" Ann inquired.

"To Mrs. White's," said Florie. "I'm going to ask her to bring little deaf-and-dumb Tommy."

Florie made her errand known to Mrs. White, and left, saying: "Bring him at three o'clock tomorrow, please."

"Now for home!" said Florie. She ran to her room the moment she arrived and wrote this little note: "Florie Swift sends her compliments to Mrs. Swift, and would be pleased to have her company tomorrow afternoon."

"Ann, please take this to mamma, and wait for an answer."

Ann soon returned with a small piece of paper, on which was written: "Mrs. Swift accepts with pleasure the invitation for tomorrow afternoon."

The next day was bright and clear, and as three o'clock drew near, Florie began to arrange her table for the guests on the green lawn. A large dish of strawberries stood in the center, on one side a large cake, and on the other a plate of biscuits. A small bouquet of choice flowers stood by each plate.

"Your company is coming," said Ann, who was helping Miss Florie.

Sure enough, there was old nurse with her walking stick, and Jamie on the shoemaker's back. Blind Mary was the next to come, and soon Amy and little mute Tommy appeared. Seating old nurse in a large chair brought out especially for her, Florie put the rest of her guests on her right and left. Mary smelled the flowers, and was delighted with them. Mrs. Swift now came into the yard, looking somewhat astonished at the company. She greeted each one pleasantly, and sat at the head of the table.

When dinner was over, Mrs. Swift invited everyone to the parlor, where she played and sang for them. Each one had a bouquet to take home, and when they left they said, "Thank you," over and over.

When they were alone, Mrs. Swift asked Florie why she had invited these friends to her party.

"Mother, our teacher told us last Sunday that God said, 'Feed the hungry, lead the lame, and help the needy,' or something like that. Did I do right, mother?"

"Yes, daughter. I'm happy that you thought of others. He who gives to the poor lends to the Lord."

The Hard Way

"FRANK, I have one more errand for you; then you may go and play the rest of the afternoon."

"Yes, father, thanks. What is it you want me to do?"

Frank's father went behind the counter and drew out a little drawer. The man handed his son a silver dollar and said: "You may carry this to Widow Boardman. Be careful not to lose it."

"I'll be careful," promised Frank, and then went out the door.

It was the first day of vacation. The boy felt happy as he trudged along the road. He was thinking of the good days ahead—two weeks and no school! Perhaps the pleasant day, the fresh air, and the sunlight had something to do with making him happy. Something else helped to make Frank happy, although he was not thinking about it. He had tried his best to do right. It makes a wonderful difference when we know we are doing our best.

Mrs. Boardman lived some distance up the road. Frank had already passed the schoolhouse, and the little pond, and was passing the willow grove, when suddenly he decided to make a whistle to blow along the way. So, putting the dollar in his jacket pocket, he climbed over the fence and cut several willow twigs. He went along with the twigs in his hand, until he reached a log lying on a grass plot by the roadside. Here he sat down and made two whistles. They sounded wonderful to Frank's ears.

As he shut the widow's gate, Frank put his hand in his

pocket to take out the dollar, so that he might have it ready to hand her when she came to the door. It was not there. Thinking he had felt in the wrong pocket, he put his hand in the other, fully expecting to feel the dollar between his fingers. *It was not there.*

Frank felt alarmed. Could he have lost it? He searched carefully in every pocket, but the dollar was lost. He turned around and went slowly back, looking carefully along the road for the lost dollar. He searched around the log, in the willow grove, by the roadside, every step of the way, but no dollar was to be seen. He went over the road again with no better success. At length he sat down upon the log to consider what he should do.

The dollar was lost, there was no doubt of that. His father had told him to be careful, and he had not been. Now what should he do? His first thought was to go back to the store and tell his father all about it. This would be the right way; but he disliked to go, for he knew his father would blame him for his carelessness.

Frank decided he would not go to his father then. He would go and play with the boys awhile. Perhaps his father would never know. At any rate he would not tell him at once. So he got up from the log and walked slowly toward the schoolhouse playground. Soon he was playing with the boys.

In the evening Frank went home and sat down at the supper table with the family. Soon after the blessing had been said, while his brothers and sisters were talking with each other about what they had been doing through the day, father turned to him and said: "O Frank, did you carry the dollar?"

"Yes, sir," answered Frank promptly.

The question was asked so suddenly that he had no time to make up his mind what to answer. He felt less like telling the truth than he had at first. It seemed too hard. He thought to take the easier way by answering "Yes." The easier way! Poor boy, he had not learned yet that it was the hard way.

Soon after supper Frank went upstairs to bed. When he said his evening prayer he did not feel that God was listening to him, and he passed a restless night.

In the morning he woke up to find the sun shining into his room. Leaping out of bed in high spirits, he began to dress. Suddenly he thought of the lost dollar, and this blotted out all his happy feelings.

The day went by slowly. Frank was troubled by the fear that father would find out about the lost dollar; yet he found it harder every hour to make up his mind to tell what had happened.

In the evening Frank could endure it no longer. The easy way had indeed become the hard way. While sitting in the front room he made up his mind to go and tell the matter. He started toward the study, where his father was. Every step in the right direction gave him new strength. He opened the study door and came to the table where his father sat writing.

"Well, Frank," father said kindly, "what is it?"

"O father," said the boy, but he could not go on. He bowed his head upon the table and sobbed.

In a few minutes Frank raised his head, and began again: "I want to tell you father"—but it was too much.

"Wait a minute, Frank. Let me tell you first," said father. "You want to tell me that you did not carry the dollar to Mrs. Boardman, that you lost it on the way, that last night you told a lie about it, that you felt wretched all the time. You wanted to tell me, but you did not dare. Is that it?"

"Yes, sir," sobbed Frank.

"You wanted to take a way easier than the right way, yet you have found it a great deal harder."

Frank knew that was true. He saw that he might have spared himself a great deal of uneasiness and sorrow by choosing the right way.

To help Frank remember, it was decided he should earn a dollar as soon as he could and take it to Mrs. Boardman. Frank set about earning his dollar, and before vacation was over, he carried it with a light heart to Mrs. Boardman.

The strangest part of the whole matter was that while Frank was returning from Mrs. Boardman's his shoe struck something hard; he looked down and saw the dollar he had lost!

Rose's Revenge

"BERTIE, here's your hat again tossed down behind the couch on the porch, instead of being hung up in the closet. Soon you would have called the family to help you look for it. Come and pick it up. I am going to require you to stay indoors all day the next time your hat is out of place. Remember."

Bertie's mother spoke emphatically. Bertie, a little sheepishly, said to himself: "I had better try to remember. Mother means it; she doesn't often speak so seriously."

The boy was in the children's room, busy painting with his new box of colors. Rose, his little sister, stood by, watching him with admiring eyes. It was fun for a while; but Bertie tired of it by and by, and leaned back in his chair, wondering what to do next. Presently a bright thought struck him, and he jumped up.

"Rose, you put away those things for me, won't you?" he asked. "I haven't time."

"Where are you going all of a sudden?" asked Rose, beginning to pick up the paint brushes and color box.

"Oh, out with my sled! I promised Jimmy Lane and Ned Wheeler to go coasting with them this morning. I forgot about it until this minute. I wonder where my hat is."

"O Bertie, may I go with you?" begged Rose. "I'll clean this all up for you. I won't be a minute. Mother said I might go with you the next time you went to the hill, if you'd take care of me. You will, won't you, Bertie?"

"Not this time," answered her brother, looking under

"Oh, boy," cried Bertie, jumping with delight, "the Brown's big sleigh! Think, Rose! Buffalo robes and bells!" Then Bertie remembered that his hat was lost!

chairs and tables for his hat. "Do you suppose a fellow wants to be bothered with a girl to take care of when he's going in for fun?"

"I think you might take me," persisted Rose. "The other boys take their sisters, and I haven't had a good ride all winter. Please, Bertie. I'll help you find your hat."

"Thanks, but I've found it myself. For a wonder, it was on the hatrack." Before Rose could put in another word, Bertie was off.

Poor Rose stood looking after him blankly for a moment. Then her face grew hot with anger. "He's a selfish boy," she said angrily, "and I know what I'll do."

Now, Rose didn't know exactly what she would do,

and by the time her brother came in to dinner, she had quite forgiven him. She remembered it again the next day, though, when mother, coming into the children's room, said: "Quick, children, get ready. Mrs. Brown has called to offer me a sleigh ride, and she says there is room enough for you. But hurry, the horses mustn't stand waiting in the cold."

"Oh, boy," cried Bertie, jumping up in delight. "The Browns' big sleigh! Think, Rose! Buffalo robes, and bells! Where in the world is that hat now?"

Rose was putting on her woolen jacket and getting her mittens and her hat. She was so busy she had not heard what her brother was saying; and he, disgusted at seeing her all ready, broke out in loud reproach.

"Yes, that's all you care, you selfish thing," he cried. "You're all ready, and you don't care whether I have to stay or not. I haven't had a good sleigh ride this whole winter. Where is that old hat?"

"I know where his hat is. I saw it fall behind the big chest a little while ago. I suppose if I didn't tell him, and made him stay home, it would be my revenge." Rose looked a little triumphant at her brother. Then she said: "Hurry on your coat and mittens. I'll find your hat." She ran to the chest, and came back as her mother appeared at the door.

Bertie looked a little sheepish as he followed his mother and sister out to the sleigh, and all he said was a hurried whisper: "You're a good girl, Rose." He said to himself, quite in earnest this time, that he had been a selfish, careless boy, and that this sort of thing had to be changed right now. Rose's "revenge" had worked.

Aunt Jane's Party

ALMOST everyone in town knew Aunt Jane. She was aunt to a dozen or more boys and girls in particular, and to all the rest in general. Aunt Jane bestowed a great deal of care and thought on her relatives, and all the time they did not claim was devoted to helping others. It was a wonder to all how she accomplished so much. She kept house by herself in a quiet way, yet not exactly alone. Children and poor persons not happy at home sought her home, where they were sure to receive sympathy in all their troubles.

Well, I had almost forgotten that I was going to tell you about Aunt Jane's party.

She was always doing "something queer," as the people called it; but, for all that, everyone loved her and approved of everything she did. Now, the party was to be on Wednesday afternoon, and the invitations were given out several days before.

Some children who had no brothers or sisters felt quite slighted because they were not invited, for she invited by pairs, but only two from any one family, even if there were a dozen children. The children's parents thought it a strange thing to do, but said there was probably a reason, if Aunt Jane did it that way.

The long-expected day arrived. There were about twenty boys and girls at the party. They played games and had exciting contests.

After the refreshments, the children were invited to look at colored pictures through a viewer that enlarged the pictures. Only one child could see the pictures at a time. The first boy rushed eagerly toward the chair, fearing that someone would be there before him. The rough push he gave his sister hurt her, and she, provoked by it, pulled his hair.

The last to see the pictures were a brother and sister named Charles and Mary Ellis, ten and eight years old. Charles and his sister had waited patiently until the last. Then, seeing that it was their turn, Charles placed the chair in the best light, and said: "Now, Mary, it is your turn."

"Oh, no!" she said. "You look first. I am in no hurry."

Someone by their side said: "You may take it home and look at it as long as you like."

Looking up, the brother and sister saw Aunt Jane smiling at them. "I had intended to give a present to every brother and sister who did not get provoked with each other," she said; "but I have watched all of you, and have noticed that Charles and Mary Ellis are the only ones who have not shown signs of selfishness. This present is a reward for your kindness. Do you think I have given it to the two who are most deserving?"

"Yes, yes!" they all exclaimed. We hope they resolved to treat each other more kindly in future.

Into the Sunshine

"I WISH father would come home." The voice of the boy who said this had a troubled tone.

"Your father will be angry," said Aunt Phoebe, who was sitting in the room reading a book.

Richard raised himself from the sofa where he had been for half an hour, and with a touch of indignation in his voice, answered: "He'll be sorry, not angry. Father never gets angry."

"That's father, now!" He started up after the lapse of nearly ten minutes, as the sound of a bell reached his ear, and went to the door. He came slowly back, saying with a disappointed air: "It wasn't father. I wonder what keeps him so late. Oh, I wish he would come!"

"You seem anxious to get into deeper trouble," remarked the aunt, who had been in the house for a week only, and who was not sympathetic toward children.

"I believe, Aunt Phoebe, that you would like to see me whipped," said the boy, a little indignant; "but you won't."

"I must confess," replied the aunt, "that I think a little whipping would not be out of place. If you were my child, I am quite sure you would not escape."

"I am not your child, and I do not want to be. Father is good, and he loves me."

Again the bell rang, and again the boy left the sofa and went to the door.

"It's father!" he exclaimed.

"Ah, Richard!" was the kindly greeting, as Mr. Gordon

took the hand of his boy. "But what is the matter, my son? You don't look happy."

"Won't you come in here?" Richard drew his father into the library. Mr. Gordon sat down, still holding Richard's hand.

"You are in trouble, my son. What has happened?"

Richard's eyes filled with tears as he looked into his father's face. He tried to answer, but his lips quivered. Then he opened the door of a glass case and brought out the fragments of a broken statue which had been sent home only the day before. A frown came over Mr. Gordon's face as Richard set the pieces on a table.

"Who did this, my son?" was asked in an even voice.

"I threw my ball in the room once—only once, in forgetfulness." The poor boy's tones were husky and tremulous.

For a little while Mr. Gordon sat controlling himself and collecting his disturbed thoughts. Then he said cheerfully: "What is done, Richard, can't be helped. Put the broken pieces away. You have had trouble enough about it, I can see. I will not add a word to increase your distress."

"Oh, father!" And the boy threw his arms about his father's neck. "You are so good."

Five minutes later Richard entered the sitting room with his father. Aunt Phoebe looked up expecting to see two shadowed faces, but she did not find them. She was puzzled.

"That was very unfortunate," she said a little while after Mr. Gordon came in. "It was such an exquisite work of art. It is hopelessly ruined. I think Richard was a naughty boy."

"We have settled that, Aunt Phoebe," was the mild, but firm, answer of Mr. Gordon. "It is one of our rules in this house to *get into the sunshine as soon as possible.*"

Into the sunshine as quickly as possible! It's the best way!

Lily May's "Good Time"

"OH, DEAR! I wish I didn't have to mind mother. When I grow up and have a little girl, I'll let her do as she pleases. If she wants to go out to play after school, I won't make her come straight home."

So said Lily May as she walked slowly toward school, feeling much abused because mother thought it was not safe for a child who had just recovered from a fever, to play in the brook that afternoon.

At home, mother said to herself: "I wonder if it would be safe for Lily May to play in the water. I was sorry to disappoint her, but I was afraid she would get cold. I think that tomorrow I shall give her permission to do as she pleases. That will let her see if she is as happy as she thinks she will be."

That night Lily May came home and began to fret. "I know I would not have caught cold playing in the brook," she whined.

"Tomorrow you may do as you please in everything, Lily May," said mother.

"Do you really mean it?" exclaimed the girl joyfully.

"Certainly, my dear."

"Oh, won't I have a wonderful time! How I wish it were tomorrow now!"

The next morning after breakfast Lily May said: "Now, mamma, I don't believe I'll go to school today."

"Do as you please, my dear," said mother.

The girl went outdoors, and presently mother saw her

(49)

Lily May sat in the swing wishing she had more to do. She decided to go into the house and get a piece of cake. Somehow it didn't taste good.

swinging under the tree. In about half an hour she reappeared, saying: "Mother, will you please give me something to eat?"

"Take anything you please," replied her mother. Lily May helped herself to a generous slice of fruit cake.

The morning hours dragged heavily for the girl. She tried one pastime after another, but found that play alone was not desirable. In fact, she would have been glad if her mother had given her some work; but she was too proud to acknowledge herself wrong and ask for some task.

After dinner she said: "I believe I'll go to school this afternoon, but don't be worried if I don't get home until suppertime."

"Very well," said her mother, smiling quietly.

After school, some of Lily May's friends said: "Come with us, Lily May, and wade in the brook; you don't know what fun we have."

The girl hesitated. Something within her told her she ought not to go; but, stifling the little voice, she hurried after the girls. Somehow she did not enjoy the wading as much as she had expected. The girls spattered water over her; and at last, one of the larger girls, for the fun of it, pushed her down into the water. Then she began to cry, and her classmates called her a crybaby and told her to run home to her mother. This she did willingly; and just before dark her mother saw a forlorn-looking little girl, her wet clothes hanging closely about her, coming to the front door.

What do you suppose her mother did then? Did she refuse to help her? Did she say that Lily May had done as she pleased all day, and might do as she pleased about getting warm and dry? No, indeed; she helped the girl change her wet clothes for dry ones, and gave her a hot supper. Then she wrapped her up warm and cozy in her bed. As mother was bending over her for a good-night kiss, Lily May threw her arms around her neck, and said: "I think it was good of God to give little girls mothers to take care of them, for they know so much more than children."

Paul's Canary

"I DON'T see why I was made this way. I was such a sickly baby, everyone thought I would die. I wish I had—" Paul paused when he thought of his weary mother and how happy he would be when she came home.

He was crouching on a seat by the one window in the room, looking out at the tall buildings and the wet boards of the near-by houses. Sometimes, leaning out far enough, he could see the paved yard, with its pile of boxes and rubbish.

Paul was far from strong. His deformed legs could hardly carry him about.

"I'm of no use at all," cried Paul. "I'm only a trouble to mother. I don't believe there is another creature in the world as helpless as I am."

As he spoke, a gust of wind shook the loose sash and blew the rain furiously against the panes. The blinds next door rattled as the storm seemed to gather force and beat against the window. Then Paul started forward with breathless curiosity to examine a little dripping object that the wind had blown onto the ledge by the window. It was a bird, apparently helpless, scarcely fluttering as it clung feebly to the stone.

"Oh, poor bird, I'll bring you in!" cried Paul. Opening the window, he gently reached out his hand. In his haste he forgot to fasten up the sash and it pressed heavily on his shoulders. The wind blew his hair into his eyes and the rain drenched him; but he did not worry about this, his only thought was for the weak creature he hoped to rescue. The

Paul watched the bird flutter on the window ledge. It seemed that the storm was determined to snatch the bird away before he could lift the window.

storm seemed determined to snatch the bird away before he could reach it. At last, however, he gathered the wet bird in his hands and drew it into the room. Before he thought of changing his clothes, he wiped, stroked, and blew the bird's feathers, trying to fan the spark of life.

The bird lay in Paul's hands hardly moving. Slowly it began to revive and to pick at its feathers. Then Paul considered himself. He had no other pants and jacket, so he wrapped himself in a blanket, taking his new pet under its folds. In the warmth and darkness, it slept. Paul, with a new feeling of content, watched it until he, too, fell asleep. When his mother came home, she feared he was sick; but on turning back the blanket, she was greeted by a lively chirp from the bird, which was now dry and comfortable. The little fellow displayed a handsome suit of black and yellow. One of his wings was injured, and parts of two toes were gone; but he was bright and chirpy and very hungry.

"Why, Paul, where did this come from?"

Paul related the rescue, and ended by asking: "Isn't he pretty?"

"Yes; but he must have some seed. I'll see if they won't give me a bit downstairs," said mother.

Soon she returned with some birdseed, and, to Paul's satisfaction, the bird began to eat. A little water in a cup served him for drink, and he slept on a stick that Paul balanced between two chairs.

In the days that followed, Paul no longer complained or felt discouraged while his mother was absent earning their living. Pet, as he named the bird, was his playmate. Paul taught the canary to take seed from his lips, to lie dead at a word of command, and to pull his master's hair or eyebrows to get attention.

Now, the birdseed that mother had borrowed soon disappeared, and Paul wondered how to get more. It would not be fair to use mother's money. Could not he earn some? He thought and thought.

The window next to his room jutted out so that he often saw Mary sitting at her work. She was sorry for the lame boy, and spoke to him. He made up his mind that she might help him. One day, as she sat plying her nimble fingers, he called: "Mary, please. What do you call your work?"

She looked up and smiled. "Tatting."

"Is it hard to do?"

"Oh, no! It's easy; you could learn it."

"Could I make enough to buy Pet some seed?"

"Why, yes; do you want me to teach you?"

"Oh, do!" cried Paul eagerly.

"I'll come in tonight."

So she did. Paul's fingers were straight and strong and he had a will to learn. Pet tried to investigate the process, pulling the thread; but Paul sent him to bed, and worked away until he could make the stitches as Mary did.

"I'll sell it for you at the same place I take mine; and if you are industrious, you'll more than buy Pet's seed—a cage, too, perhaps."

"Oh, he doesn't want a cage."

After that, Paul sat in his window as busy as anyone. He was happy over his work; and when a few pennies were left over after buying the seed, and he could buy some fruit for mother's lunch, he was as happy as any other child. Mother declared that her son was growing straighter, and someday he would be strong and would take care of her.

Some months after Paul rescued Pet, he was wakened by feeling something on his face. As he opened his eyes, he felt Pet pulling his hair with such strong tugs that it was far from pleasant. The morning light was stealing into the room, its gray cold making everything look dim and strange. Pet pulled and tugged at his master's hair.

"It's not day," said Paul, trying to send Pet away; but the bird would not go. Finally, Paul had to get up and put the canary on his perch. As his hand touched the wall, he noticed it was quite hot. Pet refused to stay on his perch, clinging instead to his master's shoulder.

"Mother," cried Paul, "mother, wake up!"

His mother was weary, and made no reply. As Paul listened, he heard the roar of fire and smelled the smoke.

Springing on his mother's bed, he wakened her and told her of the danger. She ran to the hall and aroused their neighbors; and in a moment the large house, with its many families, was in confusion. The next room was in flames. The fire had started from some clothes that were hung too near the stove; and if it had not been for Pet's alarm it would have been serious. As it was, the firemen came and soon extinguished it, though Paul's room was badly burned and he was obliged to sit with Mary the next day.

Everyone in the house came to see the lame boy and the canary that had saved their property and perhaps their lives. Paul was praised; and so many people wanted Pet, that Paul was afraid they would carry him off. Then came the man who owned the house, and he told Paul that he had saved him many thousand dollars, and asked him what he would like to have. Paul's face flushed, and then he timidly said: "Some crutches, sir, so that I can go into the street."

"You shall have them," replied the man. Paul's mother received a sewing machine, so that she did not need to go out to work; and Pet had a comfortable cage to sleep in, and all the seed he could eat.

Bertha's Queer Graveyard

BERTHA DICKINSON was a decided enemy of tobacco. She used to say she hated it. Now hate is a strong word, I know. My mother has often said to me, "My dear, you must hate nothing but sin;" and I never use the word without thinking of her advice. But I think, as Bertha did, that it is quite proper to say hate in speaking of tobacco, for it is a poison, and it injures more people than most folks are willing to believe. And then it is so nasty! There, that is another word my mother never liked to hear me use. She said it isn't a "pretty word." But I think it fits tobacco; and Bertha always thought so, too.

Bertha was a queer child. She never acted like other children, but had a way all her own, which sometimes made folks laugh, and sometimes cry, and always made them shake their heads, and say: "What an odd little girl Bertha Dickinson is!"

She took a notion into her head one day that she would have a little graveyard all her own. There was a piece of ground in the garden behind the house where nothing was planted. A long row of blackberry bushes hid this corner from the house, and she used to go down there to play. It was one day after she had been to visit Thomas Hill, the village undertaker, that she got the idea of having the graveyard. She went straight off to the woods, and brought home four pretty little trees, which she planted in the four corners of the lot she had chosen; and then, thinking it best to get permission to use the ground, she went to find her father.

"Daddy! Daddy!" she called aloud, as he and several men were threshing grain in the barn. "Will you give me the northwest corner of the garden?"

"The what, child?"

"The northwest corner of the old garden. It is bounded on the north by the old apple tree, east by the walk, south by the blackberry bushes, and west by the sweet-corn field."

There was a general laugh at the conclusion of this speech. Mother and Hapsey came out to see what was the matter.

"You needn't make fun of me," exclaimed Bertha. "I tried to be particular, so I could save you the trouble of going to see the spot."

"Bertha wants me to deed her the northwest corner of the garden, mother," said Mr. Dickinson. "Are you ready to sign the papers?"

"What do you want it for, my dear?" asked mother. "Are you going to build a dollhouse?" Her mother knew that that particular spot was her little girl's favorite resort. She was quite unprepared for the answer, and for the roar of laughter, which was repeated as the child looked up and replied:

"I want it for a graveyard, mother."

When father had recovered the power of speech, he pursued his inquiries further. "What are you going to bury, dear?"

Quick as a flash of light, Bertha picked up her father's pipe, which lay on the wooden bench by the door. "This first," said she, and off she ran.

So quick was her motion and the words that accompanied it, that no one saw what she had done. But when the day's work was finished, and the farmer was ready for his evening

As Bertha sat on her father's knee, she said: "I didn't want you to die as Mr. Thurston did." Her father smiled and agreed to leave the pipe buried.

smoke, the pipe was missing and could not be found.

"Where is my pipe? Who has seen my pipe?" shouted father in no very pleasant tones.

"I buried it, daddy, in my new graveyard," said the child coolly. "Come and see."

The heavy steps of the tired man and the light trip-trip of the little girl's feet fell together on the garden walk as they proceeded to the northwest corner of the garden, where Bertha pointed to a neat little mound. At the head of it was placed a bit of shingle with the inscription:

"HERE LIES
MY FATHER'S PIPE.
REST FOREVER."

The astonished parent was at a loss for words. He did not know whether to laugh or to be angry. Finally he concluded to do neither, but to try to get at the child's meaning in all this. So, sitting down on an overturned wheelbarrow, he took Bertha on his knees and began to question her. "Why did you do this, child?"

"Because, daddy, I didn't want you to die, as Mr. Thurston did. It's a fact, daddy," seeing a smile gathering on his face. "I heard Dr. Bell say so when we were coming from the funeral. Miss Stevens asked him what was wrong with Mr. Thurston, and Dr. Bell said: 'Pipe, Miss Stevens, pipe. He smoked himself out of this world and into—well, Miss Stevens, I can't say exactly where he has gone. If folks get so used to their pipes here in this world, I don't see what they're going to do in the other. It seems to me they'll want to keep up the smoking. I'm almost sure they can't do it in heaven, for you know, Miss Stevens, heaven is a clean place, and there is not going to be anything there that defiles.' So, daddy, I thought I'd dig a grave and bury the old pipe. You won't dig it up, will you?"

The farmer held his peace for a few minutes. Then he said slowly, but firmly: "No, Bertha, your father is no grave robber. I shall miss the old pipe; but I suppose I must say about it as we do about everything that's put in the grave, 'Thy will be done.'"

"That's good," said the child, with a kiss.

"Was that what you wanted this great graveyard for?" asked father, smiling again, and seeking to divert the conversation which he feared might get beyond his depth. "Was it only to bury that old pipe?"

"No, indeed," exclaimed Bertha earnestly. "I'm going to bury other things here, too. I expect I shall have a funeral almost every day. I'm going to bury old Auntie's snuff next."

"How will you get it?"

"Oh, I'll get it! I'll manage, daddy. And then there are Joe's cigarettes, and Uncle Ned's cigars."

Bertha proved to be a busy little undertaker, and before the week had passed more than a dozen items had been buried in the new cemetery. The graves were all made evenly, side by side, exactly the same size, nicely rounded and turfed. At the head of each was a tiny board on which was printed some simple epitaph. These headboards cost the girl a great deal of time and labor. On one was: "Auntie's Snuffbox. Closed Forever." On another: "Joe Tanner's cigarettes. Lost to view." On the next: "Cyrus Ball's Cigar. Burned out."

The northwest corner lot was finally full. More than sixty neat little graves were there in rows. The apple tree spread a friendly shade over the spot, and the blackberries ripened beside them; and many and many a visitor was taken slyly down the garden walk to see Bertha's graveyard. But the best part was that for every mound in that quiet spot, there stood a man or woman redeemed from an evil habit, a living monument above it, and all alike bearing testimony to the faithfulness and perseverance of a girl who loved purity and good health.

The Boy Who Took a Boarder

ONCE upon a time, about two hundred and fifty years ago, a boy stood at the door of a palace in Florence, Italy. He was a kitchen boy in the household of a rich and mighty official. He was twelve years old, and his name was Thomas.

Suddenly he felt a tap on his shoulder. He turned around and said in great astonishment: "What! Is that you, Peter? What has brought you to Florence? How are all the people in Cortona?"

"They are all well," answered Peter, who likewise was a boy of twelve. "But I've left them for good. I want to be a painter. I've come to Florence to learn to paint. They say there's a school here where people are taught."

"But have you any money?" asked Thomas.

"Not a penny."

"Then you can't be an artist. You had better be a servant in the kitchen with me, here in the palace. You will be sure of something to eat, at least."

"Do you get enough to eat?" asked the other boy reflectively.

"Plenty, more than enough."

"I don't want to be a servant; I want to paint," said Peter. "But I'll tell you what we'll do. As you have more than you need to eat, you take me to board, and when I'm a grown-up painter, I'll settle the bill."

"Agreed!" said Thomas, after a moment's thought. "I can manage it. Come upstairs to the garret where I sleep, and I'll bring you some dinner by and by."

So the two boys went up to the little room among the chimney pots where Thomas slept. It was a small room, and the only furniture in it was an old straw mattress and two rickety chairs. The walls were whitewashed.

Now the food was good and plentiful, for when Thomas went down into the kitchen and foraged, he found abundance that the cook had carelessly discarded. Peter enjoyed the meal, and told Thomas that he felt as if he could fly to the moon.

"So far, so good," said he; "but, Thomas, I can't be a painter without paper and pencils and brushes and colors. Haven't you any money?"

"No," said Thomas, "and I don't know how to get any. I shall receive no wages for three years."

"Then I can't be a painter, after all," said Peter mournfully.

"I'll tell you what," suggested Thomas. "I'll get some charcoal down in the kitchen, and you can draw pictures on the wall."

Then Peter set resolutely to work, and drew so many figures of men and women and birds and trees and animals and flowers, that before long the walls were covered with pictures.

At last, one happy day, Thomas came into possession of a small piece of money. I don't know where he got it, but he was much too honest a boy to take money that did not belong to him.

You may be sure there was joy in the little room up among the chimney pots. Now Peter could have pencils and paper, and other things artists need. By this time the boy had learned to take walks every morning. He wandered about Florence, drawing everything he saw: the pictures in the churches, the fronts of the old palaces, the statues in the square, or the outlines of the hills. Then, when it became too dark to work any longer, Peter would go home and find his dinner tucked away under the old bed, where Thomas had put it, not so much to hide it as to keep it warm.

Things went on in this way for two years. None of the servants knew that Thomas kept a boarder, or if they did know it, they good-naturedly shut their eyes. The cook sometimes said that Thomas ate a good deal for a lad of his size.

One day the owner of the palace decided to repair it. He went all over the house in company with an architect and poked into places he had not visited for years. At last he reached the garret, and there he stumbled right into Thomas's room.

"Why, how's this?" he cried, astonished at the drawings in the little room. "Have we an artist among us? Who occupies this room?"

"The kitchen boy, Thomas, sir."

"A kitchen boy! So great a genius must not be neglected. Call the kitchen boy."

Thomas came in fear and trembling. He had never been in his employer's presence before. He looked at the charcoal drawings on the wall and then into the face of the great man.

"Thomas, you are no longer a kitchen boy," said the official kindly.

Poor Thomas thought he was dismissed from service, and then what would become of Peter?

"Don't send me away!" he cried. "I have nowhere to go, and Peter will starve. He wants to be a painter so much!"

"Who is Peter?"

"He is a boy from Cortona who boards with me. He drew

those pictures on the wall, and he will die if he cannot be a painter."

"Where is he now?"

"He is wandering about the streets to find something to draw. He goes out every day."

"When he returns, Thomas, bring him to me. Such a genius should not be allowed to live in a garret."

Strange to say, Peter did not come back to his room that night. One week, two weeks went by, and still nothing was heard of him. At the end of that time a search was made' and at last he was found. It seems he had fallen deeply in love with one of Raphael's pictures that was exhibited in a public building, and had asked permission to copy it. The men in charge, charmed with his youth and talent, had readily consented. They had given him food and a place to stay.

Thanks to the interest the rich official took in him, Peter was admitted to the best school of painting in Florence. As for Thomas, he had masters to instruct him in all the learning of the day.

Fifty years later, two old men were living together in one of the most beautiful houses in Florence. One of them was called Peter of Cortona; and the people said of him: "He is the greatest painter of our time." The other was called Thomas; and all they said of him was: "Happy is the man who has him for a friend."

He was the kind boy who took care of his friend.

One Minute More

ON A bright sunny day while Ned sat at the breakfast table he tried to get his mother or sister to tell him where they were all going.

"I'm as much in the dark as you are," said Carolyn. "I think that mother was afraid I would let out the secret, for she sometimes calls me her little chatterbox. We're to be ready at ten o'clock sharp."

"Well, I suppose we'll know in a few hours. Look, here comes Charley Wood. I promised to show him something in my workshop." Away ran Ned.

The boys played together until after nine o'clock; and then, instead of going directly to the house, to be on hand promptly at ten o'clock, Ned thought: "Oh, there's time enough for me to finish my kite."

Two or three times his eyes were upon his watch; but there were a few minutes to spare, he thought. When he looked again, he was startled to find that it was three minutes past ten. By the time he had his hat and rushed to the front room, he was five minutes late, and no one was there.

He could not believe that his mother would disappoint him for such a little delay, so he called for Carolyn. Then he ran to his mother's room to see if she were there, then out the front door; but no one was to be seen.

"Why did mother not tell me where she was going? Then I might have overtaken her. Now I don't know in which direction to go," mumbled Ned.

It was because of this that his mother had not told Ned

Charley and Ned worked on the kite in Ned's shop, and the minutes flew by so fast that the next time Ned looked at his watch it was after ten.

where she was going. He was in the habit of trying to make up for lost time by hurrying at the last minute.

Mrs. Gray had planned a visit to her sister, who lived on a farm. Ned and Carolyn had once visited there and had a grand time with their cousins. They played in the hayloft, searched for eggs, helped feed the cattle, and rode the horses to water. They often begged mother to take them again; but she had many home cares and could not get away.

Poor Ned! When he found his mother and sister gone, he was a disappointed boy. Half ashamed to have Jane, the maid, see his tears or know how miserable he was, he went back to his play. He knew that if his mother returned, Carolyn would be sure to run out to the playhouse in search of him, so he stayed out there by himself until dinnertime.

Jane called Ned to dinner. She had lived in the Gray home a long time and knew Ned's one failing. She had promised Mrs. Gray not to tell him where his mother and sister had gone, until dinnertime. The woman saw the boy with sad, downcast face enter the dining room. Seeing the table set for only one person, Ned was surprised, for his mother rarely stayed away all day.

The boy sat down to his lonely meal, and when Jane came in with a piece of pie, he asked why his mother was not home to dinner.

"Oh, Ned," she replied, "your mother won't be back today, or tomorrow either—no, not until Monday morning. She and Carolyn have gone to visit your Aunt Mary."

This was too much for the youth. Dropping knife and fork, he rushed upstairs to his room, where he flung himself on the bed and cried bitterly.

When he had recovered from the first burst of tears, he remembered his mother's request "not to forget," that she should expect him "in the front room at ten o'clock precisely." Now he understood that she must have started with Carolyn to the station at the very moment the clock hands pointed to the hour. It was a good lesson. He knew his mother had not meant to be cruel to him, and he resolved to improve in promptness.

It was with bright, sunny face, from which all sadness had vanished, that Ned met his mother and sister when they reached home Monday morning. Mrs. Gray saw at once that the hard lesson she had been obliged to teach him had not been in vain.

Making Up

MRS. MORTON had noticed for several mornings that something had gone wrong with little Donna May. The child seemed as happy as usual at the breakfast table; but when schooltime drew near, she became restless. She took her hat and coat long before the hour and stationed herself at the window, looking up the street, as if waiting; yet when the time came, she went reluctantly, as though she had no heart to go.

When she came home at noon she was sadder than when she went.

"What grieves my little daughter?" asked her mother, as she came into the room.

"Oh, mother!" said Donna May, crying outright at a kind word. "You don't know!"

"But I want to know," said Mrs. Morton. "Perhaps I can help you."

"Nobody can help me," said Donna May. "Alice Barnes and I—we've always been friends, and now she's mad at me."

"What makes you think so?" asked her mother.

"Oh, I know! She always used to call for me mornings, and we were together at recess and everywhere. I wouldn't believe it for the longest time; but it's a week since she called for me, and she keeps away from me all the time."

"Now that I know what Alice has done, dear, can you think of anything you did?"

"Why, mother! No, indeed, I don't need to think. I thought too much of Alice." May cried again.

"There, my dear, don't cry. You must find out why she keeps away from you. Very likely there is something that you never thought of."

"I don't want to ask her, mother. It's her fault, and she ought to come to me."

"I fear your pride is stronger than your love for Alice," said mother. She was brushing Donna May's hair as she spoke, and she stooped to give the girl's forehead a loving kiss. Donna May knew that her mother was right, for she went straight to Alice when she saw her on the sidewalk after school, and said: "Alice Barnes, why are you mad at me?"

"I shouldn't think you would ask me, Donna May Morton," replied Alice, "when you've said such unkind things about me."

"No such thing!" said May indignantly.

"Donna May," said Alice, looking as solemn as her round, rosy face would let her, "didn't I hear you, with my own ears, telling Bess Porter that I was the most mischievous little thing you ever saw?"

Donna May looked blank for a moment, then burst into a laugh. Alice turned angrily away; but her friend caught her by the arm, and, choking down her laughter, said: "Alice, don't you know I named my new canary bird after you? I was telling Bess about her, and how she tore her paper to pieces and scattered her seeds all over the floor."

Alice stared and drew a long breath. Donna May's eyes twinkled again and both girls forgot their grievances in a peal of hearty laughter.

"There, Alice," said Donna May afterward, "if we ever misunderstand each other again, let's speak about it at once. Perhaps it will be something as funny as this."

Joe Green's Lunch

IT WAS a little past noon, and a merry group of boys were seated on the grass under the trees that shaded the academy playgrounds. A little later they would be scattered in every direction at their play, but first they must attend to the contents of the well-filled pails and baskets of lunch.

"I should like to know," said Howard Colby, "why Joe Green never comes out here to eat his dinner with the rest of us. He always sneaks off somewhere until we get through."

"Guess he brings so many goodies he is afraid we will rob him," said another.

"Pooh!" said Will Brown, throwing himself back upon the grass; "more likely he doesn't bring anything at all. I heard my father say the family is badly pinched since Mr. Green was killed. Mother said she didn't pity them, for folks had no business to be poor and proud."

"Well," said Sam Merrill, "I know that Mary Green asked my mother to let her have some sewing to do; but then, folks do that sometimes who aren't poor."

"And Joe is wearing patched pants," said Howard Colby.

"I tell you what, boys," said Will Brown, "let's watch tomorrow to see what the fellow does bring. You know he is always in his seat by the time the first bell rings, and we can get a peep into his basket before roll call."

The boys agreed to this, all but Ned Collins, who had sat quietly eating his dinner. He had taken no part in the conversation. Now he simply remarked, as he brushed the crumbs from his lap: "I can't see what fun there will be in that, and it looks mean and sneaking to me. I'm sure it's none of your business what Joe brings for dinner or where he goes to eat it."

"You're always nicey nice, Ned Collins," said Will Brown contemptuously.

Ned could not bear to be laughed at. His eyes flashed for a minute, and then he sprang up, shouting: "Hurrah, boys, for football!" In five minutes the whole playground was in an uproar of fun and frolic.

The next morning at the first stroke of the bell a half dozen roguish faces peeped into the classroom. Sure enough, there was Joe Green, busily plying his pencil over the problems of the algebra lesson. It was but the work of an instant to hurry into the cloakroom, and soon the whole group were pressing around Will Brown, as he held the mysterious basket in his hand. Among them, in spite of the remonstrance of yesterday, was Ned Collins.

"It's big enough to hold a day's rations for a regiment," said Harry Forbes, as Will pulled out a nice white napkin. Next came a whole newspaper—a large one, too; and then, in the bottom of the basket, was one cold potato. That was all. Will held it up with a comical grimace, and the boys laughed loudly.

"See here," said Howard, "let's throw it away, and fill the basket with coal. It will be such fun to see him open it!"

The boys agreed, and the basket was soon filled, and the napkin placed carefully on the top. Before the bell rang, they were on their way to class.

Ned Collins was the last one to leave the room. No sooner did the last head disappear, than, quick as a flash, he emptied the coal into the box again, replaced the paper, and half filled the basket, large as it was, with the contents of the bright tin pail that Aunt Sally delighted to store with dainties for his dinner. Ned was in his seat almost as soon as the rest, and all through the forenoon he looked and felt as guilty as the others, as he saw the sly looks and winks they exchanged. Noon came, and there was the usual rush to the cloakroom for dinner baskets; but instead of going out to the yard, the boys lingered about the door and the hall. Straight by them marched Ned Collins, his pail under his arm.

"Hello, Ned!" said Sam Merrill. "Where are you going now?"

"Home," said Ned, laughing. "I saw Aunt Sally making some extra goodies to eat this morning, and they can't cheat me out of my share."

"Ask me to go, too," shouted Howard Colby. At that moment the boys spied Joe Green carrying his basket into the schoolroom.

"I should think he'd suspect something," whispered Will Brown; "that coal must be awful heavy."

Joe disappeared into the schoolroom, and the curious eyes that peeped through the crack of the door were soon rewarded by seeing him open his basket.

"Hope his dinner won't lie hard on his stomach," whispered Howard Colby. But apparently Joe only wished to get his paper to read, for he took it by the corner, and pulled; but it stuck fast. He looked in with surprise, and then took out, in a sort of bewildered way, a couple of Aunt Sally's fat sandwiches, one of the delicious round pies he had so often seen in Ned's hands, a bottle of milk, and some nuts and raisins. It was a dinner fit for a king, so Joe thought, and so did the boys as they peeped from their hiding place. But Joe did not offer to taste it; he only sat there and looked at it. Then he laid his head on his desk; and Freddy Wilson, one of the smaller of the boys, whispered, "I guess he's praying," so they all stole away to the playground, without speaking a word.

"That's some of Ned Collins's work," said Will Brown, after a while. "It's just like him."

"I'm glad of it, anyway," said Sam Merrill. "I've felt mean all forenoon. The Greens are not to blame for having only cold potatoes to eat, and I don't wonder Joe didn't want all us fellows to know it." Will Brown began to feel uncomfortable.

"Father says Mr. Green was a brave man," said Sam Merrill, "and that he wouldn't have been killed, if he hadn't thought of everyone else before himself."

"I tell you what," said good-natured Tom Granger, "I move that we give three cheers to Ned Collins."

The boys sprang to their feet, and, swinging their caps in the air, gave three hearty cheers for Ned Collins. Even Will Brown joined in the chorus, with a loud "hurrah."

Later that day, Sam Merrill explained the whole matter to Ned; but he only replied: "I've often heard Aunt Sally say it's poor fun that must be earned by hurting someone's feelings."

The Conductor's Mistake

THE train was waiting at a station of one of our Western railroads. The baggagemaster was busy with his checks. Men, women, and children were rushing for the cars, anxious to get seats before the locomotive pulled away.

A man, carelessly dressed, was standing on the station platform, seemingly giving little attention to what was going on. It was easy to see that he was lame; and at a hasty glance, one might have supposed that he was a man of neither wealth nor influence.

The conductor gave him a contemptuous look, and slapping him familiarly on the shoulder, called out: "Hello, Limpy! Better get aboard, or the train will leave you behind."

The man made no reply. As the train started to move, the man climbed on the last car and walked quietly in and took a seat.

The train had gone a few miles when the conductor appeared at the door of the car where our friend was sitting. Passing along taking tickets, he soon discovered him. "Your ticket, quick!"

"I don't pay," replied the lame man quietly.

"Don't pay?"

"No, sir."

"We'll see about that. I shall put you off at the next station." And he seized his valise.

"Better not be so rough, young man," returned the stranger.

The conductor seized the bag, but then put it down and went on collecting fares. In a few minutes he learned to his sorrow who the old man was.

The conductor released the bag for a moment, and seeing that he could do no more then, passed on to collect the fare from the other passengers. As he stopped at a seat a few paces off, a man who had heard the conversation, asked: "Do you know who that man is to whom you were speaking?"

"No, sir."

"That is Peter Warburton, the president of the road."

"Are you sure?" asked the conductor, trying to conceal his worry.

"I know him."

The color rose in the young man's face, but with strong effort he controlled himself and went on collecting fares as usual.

Meanwhile Mr. Warburton sat quietly in his seat. None of those near him could interpret the expression of his face, nor tell what his next movement would be. He could get even if he chose. He could tell the directors the truth, and the young man would be fired. Would he do it? Those who sat near him waited curiously to see what would happen.

Presently the conductor came back. He walked up to Mr. Warburton's seat and took his books from his pocket, the bank bills and tickets he had collected, and laid them beside Mr. Warburton.

"I resign my place, sir," he said.

The president looked over the accounts for a moment, and then, motioning him into the vacant seat beside him, said: "Sit down. I want to talk to you."

When the young man sat down, the president spoke to him in an undertone: "My young friend, I have no wish for revenge. You have been imprudent. Your manner would have been injurious to the company if I had been a passenger. I could fire you, but I will not. In the future, remember to be polite to all you meet. You cannot judge a man by the coat he wears, and the poorest should be treated with kindness. Take up your books, sir. If you change your conduct, nothing that has happened will injure you."

Burned Without Fire

JOHNNY found a big brass button and set to work shining it on a piece of woolen cloth. "Isn't it bright?" he said, after working awhile. "Just like gold!"

He rubbed away again as hard as he could, then brushed the button across the back of his hand to wipe off some chalk dust. I had told him to put chalk on the cloth to brighten the button quicker.

"Ow!" he cried, dropping the button.

"What's the matter?"

"It's hot."

"Hot!" echoed Mary, laying down her book. "How can it be hot?"

"I don't know," said Johnny, "but it burned me."

"Nonsense!" replied Mary, picking up the button. "It's cold."

"It may be now," Johnny admitted; "but it was hot—warm, anyway."

"What a silly boy! You imagined it."

"I didn't," retorted Johnny.

Seeing that they were likely to do as many older people have done, dispute about a matter that neither understood, I took the button and rubbed it smartly on my coat sleeve and then put it to Mary's cheek.

"There!" exclaimed Johnny, as Mary cried "Oh!" and put her hand to her face.

"I shouldn't have thought your arm could make it so warm," she said.

I rubbed the button on the tablecloth, and placed it once more against her cheek, saying: "It couldn't have been my arm that warmed it this time."

"Of course not," observed Johnny.

"What did warm it?" Mary asked, her interest fully awakened.

"That's a good puzzle for you two to work at," I said. "Don't rub the button on the furniture, for it might scratch that; but you can try anything else."

Mary and Johnny worked for a long time, and still they were puzzled.

"Maybe the heat comes from our fingers," Mary suggested at last.

I put a stick through the eye of the button, so that it could be held without touching the hand. Then I rubbed it on the carpet, and it was as hot as ever.

"I guess it's the rubbing," said Johnny.

"A good guess indeed, for that is precisely where the heat comes from," I replied. "The simple fact that heat comes from rubbing is perhaps enough for you to know about right now."

"I thought heat always came from fire," said Mary, "or else from the sun."

"There are other sources of heat," I replied; "our bodies, for instance. We keep warm when out of the sunshine and away from the fire."

"I never thought of that," said Mary.

"Do you remember the day the masons were pouring water on a pile of quicklime to make mortar for the new house over the way? The lime hissed and crackled, sending up clouds of steam. I have a piece of quicklime here. See, when I pour water on it, how it drinks up the water and grows hot. I saw a wagon loaded with lime set on fire once by a shower of rain."

"Fred told me about that, but I didn't believe him. Who'd expect fire from water?"

"Get me a small piece of ice, and I'll show you how even that may kindle a fire."

While Mary was getting the ice, I took from my cabinet a small bottle with a metal bead at the bottom.

"Is it lead?" asked Johnny, when I showed it to him.

"It is potassium," I said. "I'm going to set a little piece of it afire with the ice Mary has brought. There."

"Isn't it splendid!" cried Mary, as the metal flashed into flame.

"You can do anything, can't you?" said Johnny admiringly. His confidence in my ability is something frightful. Really, if I were to tell him I could set the moon afire, I think he'd believe me.

"No, Johnny," I replied; "there are very few things that I can do, as you will discover in time. But now, while we are talking of heat, let me show you another way of warming things. Please fetch me that old piece of iron in the garage, Mary, while Johnny brings my hammer."

When the materials were ready, I said: "Now watch me while I pound this piece of lead, and be ready to put your finger on it when I stop."

"Does the pounding heat it?"

"It does. I have seen a blacksmith take a piece of cold iron and hammer it on a cold anvil with a cold hammer until it was hot enough to set wood afire."

"But we are a long way from Johnny's button. Can you think of any other time you have seen things heated by rubbing?"

"We rub our hands when they are cold," Mary said, seeing Fred go through these motions when coming in from outdoors.

"I've read of savages' making fire by rubbing sticks together," Fred continued.

"They have several ways of doing it—or rather, different savages have different ways. One of the simplest is to rub one stick in a groove in another, rubbing briskly and bearing down hard. There is a bit of soft pine board that I made to experiment with, the other day. See! When I plow this stick up and down in the groove, the fine wood dust that gathers at the bottom begins to smoke a little and turns black. By working long enough and fast enough, I could set the dust on fire; but it is too tiresome when a match will do as well. We get our fire by rubbing, too, only we use something that kindles quicker than wood. A single scratch on some rough surface develops heat enough to light it."

"What is it?" Mary asked.

"Phosphorus. I have some in this bottle. You rub the button, Johnny, while I take some of the phosphorus out on the point of my knife. Now touch it with the button. See! It is hot enough to set the phosphorus afire. We might light our fires that way; but it is more convenient to put the phosphorus on the end of a stick, and mix it with something to keep it from catching fire too easily. All we have to do is to rub the phosphorus point against anything rough. The friction heats it, and it takes fire.

"Did you ever hear of the traveler who was stopped by some barbarous people who knew nothing of matches? They would not let him go through their country, and while they were debating whether to kill him or send him back, he took a match from his pocket, struck it against his boot, and lighted it. To his surprise the people ran off to the village. After a while the chief man came back humbly, bringing loads of presents. He begged the traveler to go on his way in peace."

"What was the reason?"

"They had seen him draw fire from his foot, as they thought, and were afraid that he was a god who might burn them all up if they offended him."

"In God's creation we are constantly surrounded with mysteries, many of which we are not able to understand yet, but Jesus promises to explain them in the heavenly home to those who remain obedient and faithful to Him," mom told us that evening.

The Temptation

TWO boys, both about fifteen years of age, were employed as clerks in a large grocery store. Walter Hyde was the son of an invalid widow, and his earnings were her only means of support. Andrew Strong was the eldest son of a mechanic who had quite a large family depending upon him for their daily bread.

Both the boys were capable and industrious; both were members of the temperance club that had been started in their church. They had but lately been employed in business.

Walter and Andrew were good friends; but they had not long been employed in the store before they learned that Mr. Bates, the proprietor, retailed alcoholic drinks.

The two boys talked together upon the wisdom of remaining at a place where liquor was sold. They had nothing to do with the sale of the liquor, but they wondered if they should work where it was sold.

"Let us talk with our folks at home," said Walter, "they will know best. I shall do what my mother says."

"I'll ask my father and mother," said Andrew. "I don't know whether they will think that I should leave, but I know they will hesitate to have me lose my job."

"Mother," said Walter Hyde, seating himself beside her easy chair, "did you know that Mr. Bates sells liquor?"

"Why, no, my son," said Mrs. Hyde, with a startled movement; "does he?"

"Yes. I did not know it for a fact until today. What do you think about my staying there? I don't have anything to do with the liquor department, but it doesn't seem exactly right to stay where it is sold."

For a moment the mother did not answer. Poverty is a hard thing to battle with, and Mrs. Hyde knew only too well what must follow the loss of her son's job. But as she pondered, there came to her mind the memory of a boy she had known in girlhood; a brave, high-spirited lad with the promise of as noble a manhood as lay before her own son. How little a thing had wrecked his hopes and brought him to a drunkard's grave.

"Lead us not into temptation." When could those words be more fitly uttered than now?

"My son, let us pray together," said this Christian mother. Together they knelt in prayer in the cheerful firelight.

"I can answer you now, Walter. I would rather starve than have you exposed to such temptations. You may tell Mr. Bates in the morning that you cannot work for him any longer."

In his home that evening Andrew Strong asked the same question of his parents.

"You say you don't have anything to do with the liquor?" questioned Mr. Strong.

"No, sir; but I am right where it is all the time. I can't help that, if I stay there."

"If we were able to get along without your wages, I wouldn't have you remain another day; but I have so many mouths to feed, and our rent is coming due. If you leave there you may not get another job in a long time. What do you think, Anna," he inquired of his wife; "had the boy better leave?"

Mrs. Strong was worried about money, so she suggested a compromise. "Let him stay a little while," she said, "until

Walter resigned, but Andrew stayed on at the store. After a time he began to taste, and then to drink, alcoholic liquor. This led to trouble.

we get the rent paid, and meanwhile look up a new job for him. We won't have him remain longer than necessary."

The next day Walter Hyde resigned his position. Walter, when he found himself out of employment, did not sit down and fold his hands in discouragement, but went about looking for another job. He picked up a little work here and there. At last a gentleman, struck by his frank, manly countenance, and learning something of his history, interested himself in the boy's behalf and got him a job as clerk in a large manufacturing establishment, a far better position than he had before.

Andrew Strong remained in the store of Mr. Bates. "It was only for a little while," said his father and mother. They intended to find him another job as soon as possible. His father made inquiries to that effect whenever he thought it advisable, but nothing turned up. At first no apparent evils resulted from his stay. Familiarity with a danger causes it to seem less dangerous, so the family finally ceased to feel troubled regarding the temptations that surrounded Andrew.

For a long time Andrew remembered his pledge and was careful to avoid the liquor department of the grocery. But as the days passed and he grew accustomed to the sight and smell of liquor, occasionally he tasted intoxicating drinks. He no longer attended the meetings of the temperance club, for after he broke his pledge he felt that he had no right to be there. He did not have the courage and resolution to confess his wrongdoing and change his ways.

Twenty years passed. In one of our large manufacturing cities, as the wealthy owner of nearly half the mills in the place was walking along the street one day, he saw a man by the roadside drunk. He stopped to see if he could not do something for the poor fellow.

"Do you know this man?" he inquired of a mill superintendent who was passing by.

"No. He is a stranger here. He came to me yesterday morning to work in the mill. I hired him, and then he told me he had been out of work so long that he had been unable to get anything to eat. I paid him for yesterday's work to help him get something to eat; but it looks as if he spent it for liquor."

"What did he tell you his name was?" inquired the factory owner.

"Andrew Strong," was the answer.

"Is it possible!" The gentleman looked long and earnestly at the tramp and then said: "Yes, it must be he." Then, turning to the superintendent, he said: "Mr. Horton, if you will help me carry this man to my house, I will do you a good turn some day."

Mr. Horton looked surprised, but he did as his employer requested.

When Andrew Strong awoke from his drunken slumber he found himself in a well-furnished room surrounded by many conveniences. Beside him sat a gentleman whom he could not recall having ever seen before.

"Where am I? What does this mean?" he demanded as his senses returned to him. "Why am I here?"

"Andrew Strong," said the stranger, "do you remember me?"

"No, I never saw you before," was the answer.

"You are mistaken. You and I were once old friends. Don't you remember Walter Hyde, who used to work with you in the store?"

"Yes, yes," was the answer, "but are you Walter?"

"I am the same boy who talked with you about leaving the store because of the liquor sold there."

The man looked with bleary eyes into the face of his companion, and after a long pause said: "Then I suppose you are the Hyde that owns all these factories."

A pause, and then came a groan from the poor drunkard. "Oh! that my father and mother had kept me from that liquor house. That is where I went down. If I had left the place as you did, I might now be an honored and respected man."

"My poor friend, do not despair," said Walter Hyde. "It is not yet too late for you to reform. I will help you."

He did help him. Andrew Strong became a man respected by his fellows and a blessing to society.

The Two Gardens

"ARTHUR, will you lend me your knife to sharpen my pencil?" asked Mary Green of her brother, who was sitting at the opposite side of the table.

Arthur drew the knife from his pocket, and pushed it rudely toward her, saying, at the same time: "Now don't cut your fingers off."

The knife fell to the floor and Mary had trouble finding it, but her brother made no offer of assistance. He seemed engrossed in his geography lesson. At length he closed his books, exclaiming: "Well, I'm glad that lesson is learned."

"Now will you please show me how to do this example before you begin to study again?" asked Mary. She had been puzzling over a question in subtraction.

"You are big enough to do your homework, I should think," was the answer. "Let me see. What, this simple question? You must be stupid if you cannot do that. However, I suppose I must help you. Give me the pencil."

The problem was soon explained to Mary's satisfaction. Several hints given her as to those which followed prevented further difficulty. Arthur did not mean to be unkind to his sister; he loved to help her, though his manner seemed harsh and cross. Presently father sat down at the table where the children were studying.

"You are impolite, my son," he said.

"I cannot always think about manners," replied Arthur, rather rudely.

"Yet they are of great consequence, Arthur. A person

Mary and Arthur put aside their studies and listened as father told them that their manners were of great importance in making a success in life.

whose intentions are really good, and who desires to be of use to his fellow beings, will huit his chances of usefulness by unkind manners."

"If we do what is right, father, I shouldn't think it matters how we do it."

"You are mistaken, Arthur. It makes a great deal of difference. This morning I visited a poor woman in the neighborhood. I couldn't help her much, but for the little that I gave her she appeared deeply grateful. Finding that she had formerly been employed as a laundress by a man whose office is near mine, I asked why she did not apply to him for help. The tears came into her eyes as she replied: 'Indeed, sir, I know he is very kind, and he has helped me before when things went hard; but he has such a harsh way of speaking. A penny with kindness is worth a dollar from those who hurt our hearts.'

"Now, my son, I know this man to be a man of principle, but he has acquired a harsh, repulsive manner, which hides his good qualities. When you were helping your sister this evening you were unkind."

"But I did not feel unkind, father. Are not our feelings of more consequence than our manners?"

"Both are important, Arthur. It seems to me that kind feelings should produce kind manners."

Arthur thought but little more of what his father had said. He did not improve his manners, and his playfellows said of him: "Arthur Green is a goodhearted boy, but so rude and cross in his manners. One would suppose he is angry even when he is doing a favor."

Mr. Green had recently moved his family to a country home. Both Arthur and Mary liked the fresh air and the green fields. They asked their father to give them each a piece of ground for a garden and to show them how to prepare it for planting. This he agreed to do. Arthur did the most difficult work, but Mary was always ready to help. The brother and sister were fond of flowers, and looked forward to the time when they would be able to gather armfuls from their own garden. Their father gave them seeds and plants, and he helped them in the planting. Before many days little green leaves began to peep above the ground, and as the season advanced all the plants seemed to flourish.

"The seeds father gave me must have been different from those he gave you," said Arthur to his sister, as they were weeding their gardens one day.

"I suppose he thought we would not want to have the same kinds of flowers," replied Mary.

"No, of course not," agreed Arthur; "but I don't like the looks of my plants as well as I do yours. The leaves are coarser, and the buds don't look as if they would make pretty flowers."

Arthur grew more and more dissatisfied as Mary's plants were covered with beautiful blossoms, while his own had either no flowers at all, or were pale and small. Having had no experience in gardening, he could not imagine the reason and complained to his father.

"I am sorry that you are not satisfied with your garden, my son," was the reply. "The seeds that I gave you were the seeds of vegetables. When I last looked at them, they seemed to be growing fine."

"Vegetables, father!" exclaimed Arthur. "I wanted flowers. I didn't want to have a vegetable garden."

"I didn't suppose you would care for flowers, Arthur. Of what use are they?"

"They may not be of much use, father; but they are beautiful. We like to look at them and to have them to give to our friends. Are not things useful which give pleasure?"

"I think so, my son, but you seemed to have a different opinion. In preparing your garden, I avoided giving you those plants which possess any beauty, even as you avoid cultivating what is beautiful and pleasing in your manners."

Arthur was silent. He was struck with the truth of his father's words. At length he said: "Well, father, I will take good care of my vegetable garden this year. Every time I visit it I'll think of what you said. When you see better words and manners in me will you give me a garden that is beautiful as well as useful?"

"I will, son."

When another summer came, there had been a change in Arthur. The real kindness of his heart shone forth in his agreeable manners toward all around him. Flowers were blooming in his garden, and his father said: "These represent kindness and love."

Always the Bible

"**A**LWAYS the Bible!" said Horace Cooper to his sister. "Aren't you tired of it?"

"Almost," said Marian, laughing; "but still not *quite* as indignant as a boy not far off."

"Here we came down into the country to enjoy ourselves for the holidays, and instead of that—"

"Now, Horace," interrupted his sister, "I am sure you have had lots of fun. There were rides and uncle's amusing stories of his travels. There were luncheons in the arbor and walks with Charles and Fanny. Come, now, I can't let you find fault with *everything*."

"Perhaps not; but remember that on the excursion we had to sing a hymn under the trees, and to listen to a psalm."

"Yes, the sixty-fifth," said Marian.

"Well, and then in those stories of travel, uncle brings the same Book forward constantly. In the arbor don't we sing hymns and read verse by verse. In our walks, Charles and Fanny learn memory verses and ask us to do the same."

"So it is," returned the sister. "I confess that at first the reading and prayers, morning and evening, appeared strange; but now I begin to like it. Anyway, I do not wish myself back at Uncle Herbert's as I did the first day or two."

Horace and Marian Cooper were orphans under the guardianship of the "Uncle Herbert" of whom we have heard them speak. When about ten years of age, they had been sent to boarding schools in the city. A few summers

That evening in the cheerful drawing room, Mr. Loxley began the story. Everyone looked up and smiled when he began by saying: "When I was a boy—"

after this we find them spending a vacation with "Uncle Loxley down in Cornwall," as Horace always called him.

A beautiful place was Fernley, as Mr. Loxley's place was called. The house had ivied walls, surrounded by gardens.

That evening in the cheerful drawing room at Fernley, Mrs. Loxley, Marian, Fanny, Charles, and Horace awaited the arrival of Mr. Loxley. Charles has discovered that there is a particularly interesting story for this evening, and even Master Horace was ready to listen and applaud. At length Mr. Loxley entered and took his armchair.

"Bertha," he said, addressing his wife, "I have a long letter to read to you. What is the matter, Fanny? How crestfallen you look, my child! and Marian, too!"

"O father, it's our story; we thought you would begin now."

"Oh, I see,"—there was a merry twinkle in Mr. Loxley's eye as Charles explained the downcast looks. "I see," continued the man with assumed gravity, "the letter will have the goodness to wait awhile."

Everyone smiled assent. Mr. Loxley cleared his throat and the "story" began. "When I was a boy—"

Everyone looked up.

"Well, then, I will choose some less antiquated beginning. The snow lay thick on Salisbury Plain as I rode home from school on the top of a stagecoach. Dark and dismal was the night, not a star to be seen. It was such a night as would suit the adventurous Master Horace yonder. The coach was heavily laden, and the horses—we had six of them—could scarcely drag us over the road.

"Presently the guard whispered to a gentleman at his side: 'Shan't get through this without some mishap;' and, at the same instant, down went the coach in the deep snow. The passengers dismounted, the horses struggled nobly, still it was evident that, without more horses, the coach could not move. A conference was held, and it was resolved that the larger number of the passengers, with the guard, should proceed to the nearest village and send help immediately."

"But how could they find the way?"

"Hush, I am going to tell you. There was one man on the coach who knew 'every step of the road,' and, with a lantern in his hand, this man, looking at the waymarks which he so well knew, was to guide us to the village."

"That was great," said Horace, who was all attention.

"This man was called Guidewell, and an honest guide he was. In our company, hastening with us over Salisbury Plain, was a self-conceited man, Mr. Careless I shall call him, who never appealed to our guide. As for the rest of us, we followed Mr. Guidewell carefully. By and by Mr. Careless said: 'Why do you trust to this man? I believe I know the best way after all.'

" 'Have you ever been on this road before?' I asked, with schoolboy forwardness.

" 'Why, not exactly; but I'm tired of hearing your constant appeals to Mr. Guidewell. I wonder if you will join me to strike off to the left and find the way as best we can.' "

"Oh, how foolish!" cried Fanny.

"That's silly," cried Horace. "When one has a guide who knows the way, surely no one would go off alone and be lost!"

Mr. Loxley looked grave. "In vain we argued with him; in vain we called our guide and questioned him as to the safety of such a course. Mr. Guidewell asserted that the path which he pointed out was the only safe course; but Mr. Careless shook himself away, saying, 'Always this Guidewell, I'm tired of him.' "

"Uncle, the man must have been mad."

"Was he ever heard from again?" asked Charles.

Mr. Loxley still looked grave. "You are wrong," he said; "for, happily, some of the words which Mr. Guidewell uttered made a deep impression on the mind of Careless, and before he had walked a hundred yards, he returned and acknowledged his mistakes."

All brightened at this unexpected conclusion, and during the next five minutes the children expressed their opinions of the story.

"But father hasn't finished," suggested Fanny presently.

"Well, perhaps I should tell you that we reached the village in safety, and that the coach was soon out of the hole. The part of my story I want to impress on your memories is the adventure of Mr. Careless."

There was a pause, and then Mr. Loxley, in his kindest manner, said: "Horace, my boy, come here." Horace obeyed. "And Marian." Marian came to the other side. Their uncle took a hand of each.

"This morning," said Mr. Loxley, "I accidentally heard these words in my garden: 'Always the Bible; aren't you tired of it?'

"I stayed to hear no more; but I told you this story to help you. If a man refuse to be guided by the Bible, if he choose *his own path,* what shall be said of him? Will not the words uttered a moment ago express it: 'How foolish'?"

The brother and sister chose God's word for their guide, and the motto of their lives was: *"Always the Bible."*

Dishonesty

Some time ago a youth of about sixteen came from the country to Boston, to fill a subordinate situation in one of our first mercantile houses. The head of the firm received the youth in the most kindly manner, and caused his son to take the stranger around town, and show him the principal places during the afternoon of his arrival.

While amusing themselves in this way, the stranger youth told his companion that, in coming along in the train that morning, he had given a boy a bright cent for a pond lily, and that the coin having been mistaken for a five-cent, the vender of lilies had paid him four cents back as change.

The merchant's son questioned the honesty of the transaction, but the young man from the country defended it on the score of its smartness. Shocked at the absence of principle in his companion, the merchant's boy told his father of the transaction, who next morning interrogated the young man from the country concerning it, and found that he was somewhat inclined to pride himself on account of the act.

"Was the cheating of the poor boy, who, perhaps, had a sick mother to provide for by his industry, not cruel let alone its injustice?" queried the good merchant.

"It was his lookout," the boy replied.

"Was your conduct not dishonest?" asked the merchant.

"I don't know that it was. He ought to have been smart enough not to have given me the money."

"Young man," said the merchant, "I call your share in the matter stealing; and if the four cents had been so taken by me, I believe they would have burned a hole in my pocket."

The youth boldly replied, "They have not burned a hole in mine, sir."

Disgusted at discovering such moral obliquity in the young man, the merchant told him it was impossible that he could employ one who exhibited such dishonest notions concerning a small thing, for in matters of great importance the possessor of such loose ideas of honesty would most likely give way.

With much good advice the youth was sent home to his father, with a letter from the merchant relating the affair stated above, and expressing regret that the circumstance had completely shut the boy out from his confidence. So the young man lost an excellent chance of succeeding in life; but it is hoped that the lesson may teach him hereafter that "honesty is the best policy."

It certainly pays off to be honest.

The Tempting Gloves

IT was Christmas evening. In the Christmas market sparkled numberless lights, and their bright beams were beautifully reflected by the various wares which tempted and invited purchasers.

Many children passed to and fro—gazed with wide-open eyes at the wonderful array of pretty things—and some were induced, after long seeking, to spend the few pennies saved in the money box for this very occasion.

There were parents and other friends of children standing in the well-arranged shops, buying and examining the gifts with which they wished to delight their dear ones.

In the midst of the grown persons and children who thronged the market place, stood a young girl named Magdelain. She was alone, and gazed sadly, with a heavy heart, at the brilliant and beautiful array spread out on every side.

Her parents were very poor, and for this reason had placed her in the service of a lady, where she was employed out of school hours in going on errands, and in working with her needle. For her services she received small wages, which she faithfully took to her parents, who could do little for their own support, having other children to feed and clothe.

Magdelain was sent, this Christmas evening, on an errand by the lady with whom she lived. Her way led through the Christmas market. How gladly she would have purchased some little thing as a Christmas gift! Yet, for that, money was needful, and money she had none.

She thought and said softly to herself, "I could give up

playthings, or pretty things I could well use, if I might buy a warm dress, a shawl, or a pair of warm gloves."

It was very cold. Magdelain shivered, and her teeth chattered, for she was but scantily and thinly dressed. She blew on her half-frozen hands, and wrapped them in her apron.

"I do not want either cakes or candy, or dolls, or playthings. But, oh, I wish so for a pair of warm gloves!"

She drew near to one of the shops where many articles of wearing apparel were sold. The cold wind which blew the candle lights to and fro, seemed to pierce to the very bones of the poor girl, and she tremblingly drew herself together to keep warm.

On the right side of the shop, on the counter, lay a pair of warm woolen gloves, lined with soft skin. Magdelain saw them, and the longer she stood looking at them the better she liked them; they looked, too, as if they would just fit her hand.

Her gaze seemed fastened on the gloves—even from the moment she had seen them her hands felt warmer.

But buy—buy them she could not; they were well made and prettily wrought, and must be expensive.

Then came another thought to her mind, "I will secretly take them." The shopkeeper stood on the other side of the shop attending to a purchaser, and busily engaged in praising his goods. Magdelain stood alone, unnoticed, beside the gloves.

She thought and reflected—but the gloves were so pretty, and seemed so warm; her hands which she had drawn out of her apron, were quite stiff with frost.

Already she had stretched out her arm; already she was about to seize the gloves and rapidly conceal them. Her whole body was hot and cold by turns; her heart beat loudly; she could scarcely breathe; she trembled. Suddenly pealed out, with clear, startling tones, the organ of the neighboring cathedral.

It was a voice, earnest and warning, speaking to Magdelain's heart. Quickly she drew back her arm, and the gloves lay still on the counter.

As a voice from heaven did Magdelain receive the solemn organ tones; they seemed to say to her, "It is wrong that thou wouldst do. Thou shalt not steal!"

Magdelain obeyed the voice. She turned to leave the shop just as there entered a lady richly dressed, and warmly wrapped in a cloak of fur.

She examined and purchased some articles, and then took the gloves in her hand which had tempted Magdelain. She demanded the price, and purchased them. Magdelain had seen this, and was glad that the fatal gloves were now entirely removed from her eyes.

The lady turned to leave the shop, and Magdelain recognized her. She was the lady with whom she lived.

Now, for whom had she bought the gloves? Surely not for herself; she could hardly wear them! Her mind occupied with these thoughts, Magdelain went hastily from the Christmas market to attend to the errand on which she was sent.

In returning homeward again, Magdelain came through the market place. She said, as she passed the spot where she had been so sorely tempted, "Oh, what a fearful moment that was! God, I thank thee, that thou didst warn and deliver me from the danger which would have destroyed me! No! rather will I hunger and freeze than— —"

"Away with you to prison, boy! You will learn hereafter to keep your hands off! We'll soon cure you of your fancy for stealing. March!"

Magdelain was startled by these harsh words from the revery into which she had fallen.

A police officer had seized a wild, unruly boy, and was

taking him off.

Magdelain ran swiftly, with a beating heart, from the market place, and did not pause till she reached home.

She entered the room. Oh, what a surprise! The table was covered with Christmas gifts. There were pretty and useful articles—cakes and candies, clothing, and, above all, the well-known gloves.

The lady with whom she lived came kindly to her, took her hand, and said, "Dear Magdelain, because you are so honest and industrious, so kind and true, and have served me so faithfully, take from me, as an expression of my gratitude, a Christmas gift. Look! all on the table is your own; take all and be happy!"

Magdelain thanked her with tears of joy and surprise. Strangely, however, did she feel as her mistress singled out the articles, and said, "See, here is a cap, here a pair of shoes, here a shawl! and what do you say to these gloves? Do they please you? Yes, they will keep your hands very warm! Now take all these things to the house of your parents—show them what you have earned by your honesty and industry."

On her mother's neck, with sobs and tears, did Magdelain relate to her the story of her sin and temptation.

Her mother said, "Be good, my child, and pray to be kept from sinful desires; then it shall go well with you!" And at night, before Magdelain went to her bed, she sank on her knees and sent a prayer to her Father in heaven:—

"Lead us not into temptation, but deliver us from evil! Amen."

The Spider

On a hot summer day a gentleman sat down to think over a subject on which his mind was greatly troubled. He was wondering how it was that so many of his acquaintances had yielded to temptation, and been destroyed. He was wondering how the great tempter could so soon get them entangled in his nets and never let them loose again until they were ruined.

While he was thinking over the subject he saw a worm moving softly along in the footpath. He moved quietly and without fear. "Now," said the gentleman to himself, "that poor worm can go safely, though it has no reason to guide it. There lies in wait no destroyer to entangle it, while our young men, with reason and conscience, are destroyed by scores!" Just then he saw a spider cross the path about a foot in front of the worm. She did not appear to be thinking of the worm, nor the worm of her. When she got quite across the path she stopped and stood still. The worm kept on, but soon was brought to a stand by a small cord, too small for our eyes to see, which the spider had spun as she rushed before him. Finding himself stopped, the worm turned to go back. The instant he turned back, back darted the spider, spinning a new cord behind her. The poor worm was now brought up a second time, and twisted and turned every way to escape. He seemed now to suspect some mischief, for he ran this way and that way, and every time he turned the spider darted around him, weaving another rope. There gradually was no space left for him, except in the direction of the hole of the spider. That was left open, but on all other sides, by darting across or around, the space was gradually growing less. It was noticed, too, that every time the worm turned toward the hole of the spider, he was instantly hemmed in, so that he could not go back quite so far as before. So his very agony continually brought him nearer the place of death. It took a full hour to do all this, and by that time the worm was brought close to the hole of the destroyer. He now seemed to feel that he was helpless, and if he could have screamed, he doubtless would have done so. And now the spider eyed him a moment, as if enjoying his terror, and laughing at her own skill, and then darted on him, and struck him with her fangs. Instantly the life began to flow out. Again she struck him, and the poor thing rolled over in agony and died. Mrs. Spider now hitched one of her little ropes to her victim and drew him into her hole, where she feasted at her leisure, perhaps counting over the number of poor victims whom she had destroyed in the same way before.

When I see one disregarding his father and mother, and doing what he knows will grieve them;

When I see one occasionally going to the oyster cellar, and to the drinking saloon, in company;

When I see one going to the theater, where nothing good, but all evil, is displayed;

When I have reason to suspect that he takes money from his father or his employer, which is none of his, but which he hopes to replace—

Why, I always think of the spider and her victim, and mourn that the great destroyer is weaving his meshes about every such boy, and is drawing them toward his own awful home!

The Count and the Dove

CRUELTY to animals is always the sign of a mean and little mind, whereas we invariably find really great men distinguished by their humanity.

I remember having read a beautiful story of Count Zinzendorf when a boy. He was a great German noble, and lived to do much good in the world.

One day, when he was playing with his hoop near the banks of a deep river, which flowed outside the walls of a castle where he lived, he espied a dove struggling in the water. By some means the poor little creature had fallen into the river, and was unable to escape. The little Count immediately rolled a large washtub, which had been left near, to the water's edge, jumped into it, and though generally very timid on the water, by the aid of a stick, he managed to steer himself across the river to the place where the dove lay floating and struggling. With the bird in his arms, he guided the tub back, and got safely to land. After warming his little captive tenderly in his bosom, he ran with it into the wood, and set it free. His mother, who had watched the whole transaction in trembling anxiety, from her bedroom window, now came out.

"Were you afraid?" she asked.

"Yes, I was, rather," he answered; "but I could not bear that it should die so. You know, mother, its little ones might have been watching for it to come home!"

My First Theft

MANY years ago, when a boy of seven or eight years, my home was near a beautiful village in the central part of the State of New York. Although it was but a humble cottage, the flowers and shrubs flourishing so luxuriantly under the tender care of my mother, made it seem a paradise in my young eyes, and even now I remember the home of my boyhood as the sweetest spot on earth. My father was in humble circumstances, and by close and laborious study earned the daily bread of his family, ever looking forward to the time when the reward of his labor should bring us peace and plenty.

I was an only son, and acknowledged by all to be a growing image of my father, and although almost idolized by him, his poverty prevented the gratification of very many of my childish humors, and saved me from the fate of far too many idolized children. He was a true Christian, always endeavoring to instill good and holy principles into the minds of my little sister and myself.

The distance between my father's house and the village was about half a mile; and most delightful walk it was in summer. To take the hand of my father and accompany him in his visits to the village store, listening to his stories and carrying some little parcel for my sister or mother, was one of my greatest pleasures. There was one thing, however, which I longed for more than anything else, and which I imagined would make me supremely happy. It was a jackknife. Then I would not be obliged to borrow father's every time I wished to cut a string or a stick, but could whittle whenever I chose and as much as I pleased. Dreams of kites, bows and arrows,

(106)

boats, etc., all manufactured with the aid of that shining blade, haunted me by day and night. I had asked my father to buy me one, but he could only promise to grant my request at some future time, which to me seemed ages hence.

One of these visits, the sequel of which forms the subject of this tale, I shall never forget. It was a beautiful morning in June that my father called me and gave me leave, if I wished, to go with him to the store. I was delighted, and taking his hand we started. The birds sang sweetly on every bush and everything looked so gay and beautiful that my heart fairly leaped with joy. I was very happy. After our arrival at the village, and while my father was occupied in purchasing some articles in a remote part of the store, my attention was drawn to a man who was asking the price of various jackknives which lay on the counter. As this was a very interesting subject to me, I approached, intending only to look at them. I picked up one, opened it, examined it, tried the springs, felt the edge of the blade with my thumb, and thought I could never cease admiring their polished surface. Oh, if it were only mine, thought I, how happy I should be! Just at this moment, happening to look up, I saw that the merchant had gone to change a bill for his customer, and no one was observing me. For fear that I might be tempted to do wrong, I started to replace the knife on the counter, but an evil spirit whispered, "Put it in your pocket; quick!" Without stopping to think of the crime or its consequences, I hurriedly slipped it in my pocket, and as I did so felt a blush of shame burning my cheek, but the store was rather dark and no one noticed it, nor did the merchant miss the knife.

We soon started for home, my father giving me a parcel to carry. As we walked along my thoughts continually rested on the knife, and I kept my hand in my pocket all the time, from a sort of guilty fear that it would be seen. This, together with carrying the bundle in my other hand, made it difficult for me to keep pace with my father. He noticed it, and gave me a lecture about walking with my hands in my pockets.

Ah! how different were my thoughts then from what they were when passing the same scenes a few hours before. The song of the birds seemed joyous no longer, but sad and sorrowful as if chiding me for my wicked act. I could not look my father in the face, for I had been heedless of his precepts, broken one of God's commandments, and become a *thief*. As these thoughts passed through my mind I could hardly help crying; but concealed my feelings and tried to think of the good times I would have with my knife. I could hardly say anything on my way home, and my father, thinking I was either tired or sick, kindly took my burden and spoke soothingly to me, his guilty son.

No sooner did we reach home than I retreated to a safe place, behind the house, to try the stolen knife. I had picked up a stick and was whittling it, perfectly delighted with the sharp blade which glided through the wood almost of itself, when suddenly I heard the deep, subdued voice of my father calling me by name, and on looking up saw him at the window directly over my head gazing down very sorrowfully at me. The stick dropped from my hand and with the knife clasped in the other I proceeded into the house. I saw by his looks that he had divined all. I found him sitting in his armed chair looking very sorrowful. I walked directly to his side and in a low, calm voice he asked me where I got the knife. His gentle manner and kind tone went to my heart, and I burst into tears. As soon as my voice would allow me, I made a full confession. He did not whip me, as some fathers would have done, but reprimanded me in such a manner that while I felt truly penitent for the deed—I loved him more than ever, and promised never, never to do the like again. In my father's company I then returned to the store, and on my knees begged the merchant's pardon, and promised never again to take what was not my own.

My father is long since dead; and never do I think of my first theft without blessing the memory of him whose kind teachings and gentle corrections have made it, thus far in my life, and *forever*, my last.

After my father spent some time talking to me and explaining the possible consequences of my action, I understood the seriousness of it, and I resolved that I would never again take anything that did not belong to me.

Courage and Cowardice

Boys are very apt to get wrong ideas about courage and cowardice; they often confound the two, calling that courage which is cowardice, and that cowardice which is courage. Two or three illustrations will make this plain to all our boy readers.

George came into the house one day, all dripping wet. His mother, as she saw him, exclaimed:—

"Why, George, my son, how came you so wet?"

"Why, mother, one of the boys said I 'dare not jump into the creek,' and I tell you, I am not to be dared."

Now, was it courage that led George to do that? Some boys would say it was; and that he was a brave and courageous boy. But no, George was a coward; and that was a very cowardly act. He well knew that it was wrong for him to jump into the creek with his clothes on, but he was afraid the other boys would laugh at him, if he should stand and be dared.

Edward came strutting along up to James, and, putting his fist in his face, said: "Strike that if you dare!" just to see if he couldn't get him into a quarrel. Now, which would show the most real courage, for James to give him a hit and have a brutal fight, and both get wounded, or to say, as he did: "Edward, if you want a quarrel, you have come to the wrong boy. I never fight, because it is wrong. You may call me a coward if you will, but I will show you that I have courage enough not to be tempted, by your ridicule, to do what I know is *wrong!*" That was brave and courageous.

Well, a great man, Mr. A., a member of Congress, said

something that offended Mr. B., another great man. Mr. B. sent him a note and dared him to fight; that is, he challenged him to fight a duel. Mr. A. accepted the challenge, and they met with deadly weapons and sought to take each other's life. Now, some said Mr. A. was a man of courage, because, like the foolish boy who jumped into the creek, he wouldn't be *dared*. But Mr. A. accepted that challenge, probably, through cowardice. He knew it was breaking a positive command of God to attempt to kill the man who dared him, but he had not courage enough to bear the tauntings of those who would say he was afraid to fight. He was a coward!

A good definition of courage is, *"not to be afraid to do what is right, and to be afraid to do what is wrong."* The stories of Daniel and his three friends, and of Joseph, give us fine examples of those who possessed true courage, who were not afraid to do what was right, and who were afraid to do what was wrong.

Dare to be honest, good, and sincere,
Dare to be upright, and you never need fear.
Dare to be brave in the cause of the right,
Dare with the enemy ever to fight.
Dare to be loving and patient each day,
Dare speak the truth, whatever you say.
Dare to be gentle and orderly too,
Dare shun the evil, whatever you do.
Dare to be cheerful, forgiving, and mild,
Dare shun the people whom sin has defiled.
Dare to speak kindly, and ever be true,
Dare to do right, and you'll find your way through.

The Sensitive Plant

MY mother and her three children came back to live with grandfather. The children were very glad to leave the city and go into the country, where the large green fields were, and shady trees to play under. Grandfather had a beautiful garden; he loved a garden dearly, and he had taken great pains to fill it with fine fruits and flowers. It stretched to the brink of a small creek. Here was a summerhouse covered with woodbine. It was very cool and pleasant in the summerhouse.

Grandfather gave Robert and myself a little spot for our garden. We were very much pleased to have a little garden of our own; every morning and evening we worked in it. Grandfather once said he thought it was the nicest-looking corner in his great garden. This made us very glad.

One day a gentleman came to see us from afar. He visited the garden and talked a great deal about gardens and flowers. We thought he loved them as much as grandfather and mother did. When he went away, he patted me on the head and said, "I will send you some seeds of the sensitive plant, my child, to plant in your dear little spot."

The seeds came, and mother kept them carefully for the next spring, when we took more pains than usual in making our garden, on account of our beautiful new plant. No sooner was it planted than we longed to see it up; every morning we ran to look for it. "I hope it don't mean to cheat us," cried Robert, after waiting long in vain. Mamma said she did not think it meant any such thing; perhaps it was waiting for more sunshine.

(112)

After many days, something began to turn up the earth. "It's come, it's come! the sensitive plant has come through," I cried in joy, racing to mamma's chamber; "it's got here at last; come and see, mamma." Never was flower plant watched with deeper interest.

As the weather became warmer, small branches came out of the parent stem, and grew rapidly. One day as Robert and I worked in our garden, by chance he brushed his hand rudely against it. Lo, the little leaves folded themselves suddenly together, and shrunk down towards the earth; it looked abashed and frightened. "See the sensitive plant," I cried; "Robert you have killed it." "It can't be," said Robert. We looked at it in wonder. "Let's go and tell mamma, and ask what it means." Robert ran for her. Meanwhile I hung over the plant with the greatest curiosity; it began to stir itself again.

"It's not dead, it's only terribly frightened," I cried as Robert and mother came down the walk. Then she told us it was for this reason called the sensitive plant, because it shrunk so timidly from the touch, modestly hanging down its little leaves and branches. It seems to have the power of feeling in a great degree, in this respect differing from many other plants. As we stood and looked, the little thing raised itself up and opened its leaves; mamma touched it again with her finger; it shrank away from her instantly. "This is queer enough," cried Robert, "I am glad the gentleman sent it." Robert was for showing it to everybody; indeed, he was never tired of trying its wonderful properties, and whether it did really feel or not was a question we talked over a dozen times a week. It was a wonder to all the children around. At length someone told us it would lose its sensitive power if we tried it too often. Henceforth we began to be very choice of it.

One day I came home from school very ill-humored. I ran through the long entry into the garden. Catching a view of mamma at our garden, I ran across the beet beds towards her. She was handling our sensitive plant. "Oh," I cried, "you are always hurting my sensitive plant; you shan't." She looked up into my face. "The cow has been in the garden," she said, and then arose and walked away. I bent down. Behold, the print of a cow's hoof directly on the spot where it grew; one side of it was torn and broken, but the dirt had been carefully brushed off and the stalk set erect. And mamma in her thoughtful love had gone to its help.

How had I spoken to her! how had I repaid her care! Her look of sad surprise and mild rebuke pierced my heart. I would have given anything to recall those angry words. I wanted to run and throw my arms around her neck and ask her forgiveness. Standing on tiptoe, with the tears blurring my eyes, I looked anxiously around the garden to find her. She was gone. No good opportunity came that afternoon of seeking her forgiveness, and if it had, perhaps I felt too much ashamed of my wicked conduct to speak of it. That night I lay down upon my pillow with a great weight upon my heart.

"Mamma, dear mamma, I did not mean to," I sobbed aloud when the lamp was taken away, and it was dark. Alas, she did not hear.

During the week I tried all I could to be a dutiful, obedient child, in the hope of making up for my angry words; but they had been spoken and could not be unspoken. I remembered them, if she did not. The sensitive plant never looked to me as it had done.

Twenty years passed away from that summer, and I was then away in a distant part of the land. A letter was brought to me one evening, saying that my mother was very ill. I went to my chamber with an aching heart. The thought that I might never see my mother again filled me with grief. In the night I awoke thinking of it. "Mother, dearest mother," I cried, "would that I were near you." Then came vividly to my mind the angry, unkind words I had spoken twenty years before. It added to my sorrow; I thought of all her tender love, all the happy and beautiful hours which we had passed together. I tried to comfort myself with thinking how happy I had made her, how much I had added to her enjoyments; but alas, it could not *make up* to my own heart for the angry, harsh words spoken twenty years before. I could not forget them; I could not blot them out; they came and doubled my grief. I had often remembered them before, but now they seemed sharper than a two-edged sword.

Harsh, unkind language to my mother, my dearest and best friend—she who loved me so dearly, who bore so patiently with my faults, who with such a kind and steady hand led me in right paths, who nursed me in sickness and cared for me as no one else could. I could never repay her. Even now, whenever I sit down and call to mind what a dear, good mother she has been, I weep for the sin of those wicked words. I wish I could forget them. Oh, I wish they had never been said! To this day I cannot look at a sensitive plant but with sadness. Sin casts long, dark shadows on all our pleasures.

Should any children read this story, I hope they will learn a sad and solemn lesson from it. If you would not lay up in your heart sorrows for future time, which will *never* heal, be kind, obedient, respectful to your mother, to your father. At best, you can never repay their love. Strive to do what you can. Make them happy; watch your lips lest any word escape that will wound their feelings; if once said, it can never be unsaid. Always bear in mind the command given by God himself, "Honor thy father and thy mother."

The Burnt Composition

THERE! it is finished, mamma! Will you read it over now, and see if it is correct?"

Mrs. Carter looked up from her sewing at her little girl's eager, flushed face, smiling at her earnestness.

"Let me see, dear," she said, taking the papers in her own hand. "It looks very neat."

"There is not one blot or erasure," said Nettie; "if the spelling and grammar are right, I think my chance for a prize is a good as anyone's. Mr. Mason said he would give prizes for all the correct compositions, though the writing desk is for the best one in every way. I don't think I shall get that, mamma. We all think Hattie Ross will have that, if she is only careful about her blots. She does write so beautifully; only she will blot and smear badly. I guess she will be neat this time, though, the desk is such a beauty, with a little silver plate for the name of the winner. If I can get one of the books for correct composition, I will be satisfied."

"I think you will get one, Nettie," said her mother, after carefully reading the composition. "This is correct, well expressed and very neat."

"Now, mamma, will you tie it with the ribbons for me, and I will put it away."

The precious manuscript being tied nicely with crisp, dainty ribbons, Nettie put it carefully in her desk, with a long sigh of relief. It had been a very difficult task for the little twelve-year-old girl to complete a correct and neat composition. She was not fond of writing, had hard work to put her ideas into words, and found it quite as hard to keep her sheet clean. So it was quite a triumph when the work was really completed, entirely alone, and had been pronounced worthy of a place among the prize compositions.

The little girl was still in the room where she and her sisters studied, when Amy, her cousin, nearly her own age, came in, flushed and tearful.

"Is your composition ready?" she asked.

"Yes, and mamma says it will do."

"Then you can help me with mine. I have tried and tried, and I can't write one."

"But, Amy, if I help you, you can't try for a prize. You know Mr. Mason said we must not have any help, even from our parents."

"Your mamma helped you."

"No, not one bit. She only read it when it was finished."

"But you will help me, Nettie. Nobody will ever know."

"But it will not be honorable."

Amy would not listen, however, to her cousin. She coaxed a long time, making it very hard for tender-hearted, good-natured little Nettie to refuse the request. She loved Amy very dearly, and it was her constant habit to assist her with all her lessons and exercises. Only the fact that it would be a dishonorable trick upon their teacher kept her from yielding now. Hard as it was for her, she refused upon that plea.

Then Amy grew angry, taunted her with jealousy, selfishness, and miserably mean motives, that Nettie felt were untrue and unjust. Working herself into a fury, Amy suddenly seized the precious manuscript her cousin had just completed, and tossed it upon the red coals of the open grate.

"If you won't help me to a prize, you shan't have one yourself," she cried.

"Oh, Amy!"

The cry was too late to save the treasure. Already it was curling up in the fierce heat, and a bright blaze was in a few moments all that was left of the work of many play hours.

As the flame died away in a black mass, both children stood very still, looking at the destruction one passionate moment had made. Already Amy was sorry, for her tempests of temper never lasted long, and she hoped Nettie would scold and cry, as she would have done, and then "make up." But Nettie's grief was too deep for anger. She did not speak after the first cry, but went silently from the room to lock herself in her own little bedroom, and sat down for a hearty cry.

Remember, she was but twelve years old, and had worked very faithfully for the promised reward. As the tears ran down her cheeks, her thoughts were very busy.

"I will never speak to Amy again, nor help her with a single lesson. She had no right to burn it. I would have helped her with anything else, but this would have been wrong; it would have been cheating to write this composition. I'll never forgive her, never! It was so pretty, too! And I cannot have another ready in time—there is so much to do before examination, and only one week for all. Oh dear! I wonder if Amy feels bad. I should, I know. I hope she does. Do I? Is this Christian forgiveness? Only one month since I resolved never to be bitter again, to conquer my temper, and try to be a real, true Christian, like mamma; and now I am revengeful, unforgiving, and wicked. What shall I do? I *can't* forgive Amy, I can't."

So her thoughts ran, now blaming Amy, now herself, the tears flowing fast all the time. At last the little girl, tired of crying, knelt down and said very softly the Lord's Prayer. Her sweet face was very earnest as she whispered, " 'Forgive us our trespasses as we forgive those who trespass against us.' I will forgive Amy. Help me, Heavenly Father, to forgive her, as I hope to have all my sins forgiven."

In the meantime, a very unhappy, penitent little girl was walking slowly homeward. Amy would have given all her own hard study for the other prizes if she could have restored the burnt composition. Her conscience was very sore. She knew that Nettie was right in refusing her request, and she knew that in every way she had been wrong; wrong in asking for help, wrong in getting angry, and oh! how very, very wrong in taking such a wicked revenge for Nettie's refusal! She thought of the many hours Nettie had spent trying to help her in her studies, of the many times her cousin had given up a pleasant walk or ride to aid her in a difficult sum or exercise; and before she reached home, Amy was quite as sorry and felt quite as guilty and mean as Nettie could have wished her had she been ever so revengeful.

The next morning, after Nettie had started for school, Mrs. Carter was surprised to see Amy, with a grieved face, standing before her.

"Aunt Mary," she said, trying not to cry, "did Nettie tell you about the composition?"

"Yes," Mrs. Carter said very gravely.

"Do you think she will forgive me, if I try to make up the loss, Aunt Mary? I am so sorry."

"I don't think the loss can be made up, Amy."

"I have tried to make it right, Aunt Mary. It was very hard to do, but I went to Mr. Mason this morning, and told him the whole story. He says if you will send him a note saying the composition was correct and neat, he will consider it the same as if he saw it himself. O Aunt Mary, please do! I am so miserable."

Mrs. Carter pressed a warm kiss upon the penitent little face.

"If you always atone for a fault so nobly as this, Amy," she said kindly, "you will not feel miserable long. It will be a lesson for you and help you to check the hasty temper that gets you into so much trouble. I will write the note to Mr. Mason now."

The note was soon ready, and Amy took it gratefully.

"Will Nettie forgive me now, Aunt Mary?"

"Nettie forgave you fully and freely before she slept, Amy."

"I wonder if I could be so good as that?" Amy said tearfully. "I am sure I can never be ugly to Nettie again."

When the examination day came, Mr. Mason handed each of the cousins a small pocket Bible.

"Yours," he said to the wondering Amy, "is to prove to you how much I appreciate the true penitence that acknowledges a fault at once, and tries to make amendment. Nettie earned a reward by her hard study, and she holds it in her hand; but, above all study, I prize the Christian kindness and forgiveness that kept her silent when I asked for her composition, rather than tell me how it was destroyed."

I have told you this story, little readers, because it is true, every word of it, and proves how truly the power of prayer and principle will aid us in atoning for faults and forgiving our enemies.

The Revenge

I WILL never forgive him, that I won't," exclaimed Basil Lee, bursting into the room where his eldest sister was quietly seated at work. "I will never forgive him."

"Never forgive who, Basil? my dear boy, how angry and excited you look; who has offended you?"

"Why Charles West, Alice," replied Basil, as he put his books away in their place.

"And what has Charles West done to offend you? Come and sit by me—there, now tell me all about it."

"Well," said Basil, "Mr. Raymond, who is a friend of Mr. Mathews, and is staying with him, came into the schoolroom today. He is a very nice, kind gentleman, and so he offered a half dollar to the boy who first did a sum he should give out. Five boys besides me took up their slates; he set us all the same sum, and then we all set to work. Charles West came and sat next to me, and I saw him copy down every figure as fast as I did it. When I had only one figure to do, Mr. Mathews left the room; I looked to see who went out, and when I turned to my slate again, every figure was rubbed out; I know Charles did it because he colored so. In a minute he had finished his sum and carried it up; it was first done, and correct; so he had the half dollar. I was so angry, the bell rang to go home, and I ran off directly; but I am determined to have a glorious revenge on him. Was it not provoking, Alice?"

Yes, very, dear; and what is your revenge to be?"

"Oh, I know, I will tell you; he just deserves it. Mr. Mathews has said that he will turn any boy out of the school who uses the key to the grammar exercises. Well, I saw Charles using one, yesterday, and I will tell of him; I am determined."

"Listen to me a moment, Basil. Charles is only at school for one more year; at the end of that time a gentleman has promised, if he behaves well, to place him in a situation, where in a few years he will be able to support his widowed mother. Do you think the gentleman will give him his situation if he is turned away from school in disgrace? And what would be the disappointment of his aged mother, to think that her son, who she hoped would support and comfort her latter days, had disgraced himself! Surely, it would bring down her gray hairs with sorrow to the grave."

"Oh, Alice," exclaimed Basil, with tears in his eyes, "I never thought of that. No, no; I would not ruin poor Charlie for the world."

"This would be your glorious revenge, my dear boy," said Alice, quietly.

"Oh, no, no! dear Alice, I never, never, could be so wicked as that though Charles did make me very angry at the time; but you know I should like to punish him a little for it."

"Well, Basil, I know a good way to punish him, and also to have a really glorious revenge."

"O, dear Alice, pray tell me what it is," said Basil.

"Well, do you remember the text, 'Be not overcome of evil,'—what comes next?"

"Why, 'But overcome evil with good,' to be sure, Alice. I know what you mean now."

"Well, then, think over what a glorious revenge you can have by obeying the command in that text, my dear;" and Alice left the room.

Basil did not sit thinking long before he decided what he would do. With Alice's permission, on the following day, he invited Charles West to go home with him; he was much surprised on receiving the invitation, but accepted it. They had a very pleasant evening together. Their principal amusement consisted in sailing Basil's ships on a pond in the garden; for the finest Charles expressed great admiration; but the time for his return came. Basil took him up to his play room.

"Charlie," said he, "you admired the Hero most of all my vessels; so I will make you a present of it."

"Oh, no," said Charles, stepping back, "I could not think of such a thing."

"Oh, but Charlie you must have it. I can do what I like with my ships, and I can make myself another just like it; and father says if Mr. Mathews will allow you, you can come up some day and sail it with mine, and I will teach you how to make ships, too."

Charles turned away his head to hide the tears.

"Basil," he exclaimed, as they bid each other good night, "I will never try to injure you again as I did yesterday—no, I never will. Good night, dear Basil."

From that day Charles and Basil were firm friends. Charles was easily persuaded never to use the key to the exercises again. After this he always tried to imitate his friend's example, and he gained the esteem of his master, and the love of his school fellows.

My young readers, was not Basil Lee's a glorious revenge?

The Wicket Gate

REUBEN RAYNER was a young orphan lad who was sometimes employed to take care of Farmer Aswell's flock when his shepherd had other work to do on the farm. This was a way in which the boy could honestly earn a few pence, and so help to gain his own living. Reuben was of a very reflecting mind, and many a thought would come into the orphan's brain as he sat on the long grass under the hedge, with the flock quietly nibbling around him, no sound heard but the tinkling of the sheep bell, or the hum of a bee on the wing.

There was a railway at no great distance, and now and then there would come a rattling, rolling noise, and then a roar, as a train rushed by; but the flock was accustomed to this, and the sheep scarcely raised their heads from the daisied mead on which they were grazing to listen. Along the line of railway stretched telegraph wires; Reuben could just see them above the thick hedge which shut out the railway from view. These wires were always a subject of wonder to the boy, who could not make out how messages could possibly be sent along them.

Here have I been sitting watching these lines for hours, thought Reuben one morning, and I've heard that messages by scores are being passed backwards and forwards along them every day, and yet nothing can I see. Now and then a bird perches on the wires, but of letters or words there is neither sound nor sight! It is hard—very hard—to understand! Reuben raised his eyes as he spoke far higher than the telegraph wires, right up into the blue sky flecked with many a cloud, like fleecy flocks above him. It's more wonderful still, thought the boy, how our

(124)

prayers—even prayers not spoken aloud—can pass up, up, beyond those clouds, and reach the Lord God in Heaven, as my dear mother used to tell us that they do!

It seems so strange that the great God should care to listen to what a poor boy like me can say! And yet there is his promise for it, "Ask, and it shall be given you. Seek, and ye shall find. Knock, and it shall be opened unto you." What can that word about knocking mean? Ah! it reminds one of the knocking at the Wicket Gate in the Pilgrim's Progress. Christian came to the gate, that must mean coming to the Lord; Christian knocked at the gate, that must mean praying to the Lord. Have I ever come to the Wicket Gate, have I ever really knocked?

It would be well if all young and old, would in some quiet hour ask their own hearts such a question. We cannot even begin to walk on the straight, narrow path which leads to heaven, without coming to the Lord by faith; and then our first earnest prayer is the knock of Christian. I wonder if one is knocking at the gate when asking just for anything one wants—earthly things I mean, said Reuben to himself, with his eyes still raised to the clouds above him.

Now, I want very much to get a place at Squire Elphin's, and help to look after his horses; I should like that kind of life so much better than this. I want regular work, and regular wages, and plenty of food, and not to have Aunt Poulter twitting me and my poor little sister with being burdens on her. She calls us useless mouths, and goes nagging at us as if we were lazy, when we're ready enough, I'm sure, to do anything that we can. If I could get the place at Squire Elphin's, I should soon earn enough to keep both myself and poor Grace.

I've sometimes thought of going right up to the Hall, and asking to speak with the squire himself; for I know he's looking out for a handy boy. But somehow or other

I'm afraid to go; he'd think it so bold in a poor boy like me. Reuben shook his head at the idea of venturing upon such an errand. But I can ask the Lord to help me to get the place, if it be really good for me; and I need not be afraid that He will be angry at my boldness. I can tell Him of things that I could not even tell to my sister! God, Who has all the world to care for, is yet never too busy to attend; and though He is King of kings, He does not scorn a poor cottage boy.

Reuben felt that it would be a comfort to him to pray at once to the Lord. The spot where he was appeared very quiet, being quite shut out from the railway and the meadow between by a very thick hedge. Into that retired corner of the field seldom anyone ever came but Reuben himself. The place was a great deal more private to pray in than Aunt Poulter's cottage, in which Reuben had not a corner to himself, for he even slept in the kitchen. To kneel on the grass, close under the hedge, with nothing but the soft blue sky and pure clouds above, was almost like being in church—at least so it seemed to Reuben.

Wherever a Christian earnestly lifts up his heart in real prayer, there is the Wicket Gate. Reuben clasped his hands, and sure that no one on earth could hear him, in the earnestness of his soul he prayed aloud, "O Lord! if it be good for me, let me have the place which I wish so much!" Reuben had not time to add that which should end every prayer—"for the sake of thy dear Son"—when he was startled by the sound of a very loud laugh at the other side of the hedge.

"Ha, ha, ha! there's a saint for you! Ho, ho, ho! he'll be preaching next in his smock frock, with the sheep for his hearers! he, he, he!"

Reuben knew the coarse voice of Dathan Whittle, the blacksmith's son, and the moment that he heard it sprang up from his knees, looking as awkward at being caught in the act of praying, as he might have been had he been found in that of stealing.

Dathan had been silently gliding along, at the other side of the thick hedge, searching for nests, so quietly that Reuben had not heard his approach. There was a gap in the hedge not far off, and the clumsy figure of Dathan, in his old velveteen jacket and wide-awake, was soon seen pushing through the branches and brambles, and then jumping over the dry ditch.

"What was that you was praying for?—a place? That's the right place for you, my fine fellow!" And Dathan, who was half as large again, and twice as strong as Reuben, kicked the shepherd boy into the ditch. "You'll not be such an idiot as to pray again, as if you thought that you could get anything by it!" laughed Dathan, as he watched Reuben scrambling out of the ditch. As soon as the boy, with his jacket torn, his face scratched, bruised, and half covered with mud, had got on the grass, Dathan gave a sudden whoop and halloo, and dashed at the sheep, highly amused to see them scampering off in a fright.

Happily for Reuben that Dathan had some mischief to do elsewhere, and did not remain long in the field either to jeer at him or to give chase to his sheep. After flinging a stone at Reuben—a stone which very nearly hit him on the head—as a parting salute, Dathan turned on his heel and went off through the same gap in the hedge as that through which he had forced his way before.

Perhaps, said the boy to himself, the day may come when Dathan may find that the idiot is not he who prays, but he who mocks at prayer.

On the evening of the same day, as Reuben sat in his aunt's kitchen, eating some dry crusts for his supper, and bitterly feeling that even these were grudgingly given to him, there was a tap at the cottage door, and it was opened by Blackburn, one of the railway men, who said, "Mrs.

Poulter, can you spare that boy of yours to take this telegram up to Lylow Lodge? He'll get a sixpence from Mr. Diggins for his pains."

Reuben eagerly started from his seat, and stuffed what remained of his crust into his pocket, for he had too scanty a supply of food to waste any of it. Mrs. Poulter merely looked up and observed, "When the boy's sent on errands after dark, Mr. Diggins, if he is a gentleman, will make the sixpence a shilling."

"Shall I have to wait for an answer?" asked the boy.

"You'd better," replied Blackburn; "though that paper holds, I take it, a reply to a telegram which Mr. Diggins sent this afternoon to London."

This afternoon! repeated Reuben to himself, as he took down his cap from its peg, and left the cottage with the paper in his hand. Only a few hours have passed, and here comes an answer to a message sent in some strange way along those very lines that I have been watching. No one saw, no one heard it pass; but it reached the place it was sent to, and here is the reply! And has not my little prayer reached Heaven even more quickly? and may not I too look for an answer?

The night was closing in darkly, for there were many clouds, and no moon. Before Reuben had reached Lylow Lodge, he could scarcely see two yards before him; but this mattered little, as he knew every step of his way. His reflecting mind was full of thought, as he walked along the dark road bordered by hedges, on which he could not distinguish a leaf or a twig.

I cannot see Lylow Lodge, thought Reuben, but I know that it is there to the left, and I'm sure that I'm on the right road to the place. Perhaps that's something like what we hear of in church as faith. We can't see our way to Heaven—and we can't see how prayer reaches God, or how he can make everything turn out at last for our good—we go on, as it were, in the dark; but we know that there is a hearing God, and a Heaven for those who love him, for the Bible teaches us the way to both. Ah! there's a little light gleaming before me; that must be from Lylow Lodge.

The lodge was reached, the telegram given in; Reuben received the sixpence which he had earned, and set out on his homeward way. The road skirted the park of Mr. Elphin. The ground, which was very low near the Lodge, gently rose almost all the way to Mrs. Poulter's cottage. Instead of the distant sound of waves, which he left behind him, Reuben now heard the rustle of the wind in the creaking branches of the trees.

Reuben had never been within Elphin Park,—not that its oak fence was high enough to keep out an active boy, nor that he had not longed to ramble in the only woods near, the only place where squirrels might be seen springing from tree to tree, or a whirring partridge rising on the wing. But Mr. Elphin was not one to suffer trespassers on his preserves. Reuben had often read the warning nailed to a tree: BEWARE OF STEEL TRAPS AND SPRING GUNS. Little mercy was likely to be shown to anyone trespassing in Elphin Park, especially after nightfall.

Hark! exclaimed Reuben, suddenly stopping to listen as he was slowly ascending a steeper part of the road; surely I heard something in the woods back there! It's not the rush of the wind; it's not the creaking of the branches. There again; I'm sure I heard it! It's the voice of someone in distress!

Reuben was a kind-hearted boy; he could not pass on with the moan of pain or terror sounding in his ears. He had never before trespassed in Squire Elphin's grounds, but now, quite forgetting steel traps and spring guns, and the difficulty of finding his way through the woods at night, Reuben scrambled up the bank and over the paling, and was in the park in a minute.

He had nothing to guide him but the sound of distress, and groping his way between trunks of trees, through bramble and thicket, he kept as straight a course as he could in the darkness. Pausing again to listen, Reuben heard distinctly the words, uttered in a tone of agony, "O God! have pity upon me!" It was a prayer from lips little used to praying. Reuben knew the voice of Dathan Whittle.

"Dathan, what's the matter? It's I—it's Reuben!" exclaimed young Rayner, as he pushed forward towards the spot whence the cry proceeded.

"O Reuben! for mercy's sake run to my father's; tell him to come quick—quick—and bring his tools! I'm caught in a trap; I can't get out; the iron is biting into my flesh!" the sentence ended in a groan.

"Can I not set you free?" exclaimed Reuben.

"No, no; you have not the strength. Run, run for my father—every minute adds to my torment; I can't bear it much longer. I so feared that no one would come to help me!"

And so, when he believed that no one else would hear him, thought Reuben, he began crying to God! He mocked and jeered me for thinking that I could get anything by praying, but when his hour of trouble came, even he felt that there is One above Who can hear and may help. But if we never pray to the Lord in time of sunshine, can we expect that He will answer us in time of darkness?

Reuben with some trouble regained the road, and set off at full speed for Whittle the blacksmith's home. The moon was now rising, so the boy was easily able to find his way along a road which he knew so well. Panting he arrived at the blacksmith's, where he found Whittle and his wife at supper. Reuben told them the story of Dathan's distress as well as his breathlessness would let him, and ended by begging the blacksmith to come as fast as possible to get his son out of the trap.

"Ay, ay; I'll come," said the man surlily; "but I'll give him such a thrashing as he never had in his life for ever getting into it. I'm obliged to you, Reuben Rayner, and here's a shilling for your night's work."

Reuben had the shilling, and Dathan the thrashing, for Whittle was a man of his word.

A few days afterwards Reuben got the place at Squire Elphin's, and lived in it many years, till he gradually rose to be the head man and confidential servant. If with Reuben, as with Joseph in the Bible, God made everything seem to prosper, it was because in everything Reuben Rayner looked to God. Not only every morning and evening, but whenever sorrow tried or difficulty perplexed him, Reuben turned to the Lord for counsel and help. He knocked at the Wicket Gate by prayer.

As the messages are transmitted across the telephone lines, so are our prayers conveyed to our Saviour Who answered Reuben's earnest request.

The Wanderer's Prayer

ON a cold, dreary evening in autumn, a small boy, poorly clad, yet cleanly and tidy, with a pack upon his back, knocked at the door of an old Quaker in the town of S_____, and inquired, "Is Mr. Lanman at home?"

"Yes."

The boy wished to see him, and was speedily ushered into the host's presence.

Friend Lanman was one of the wealthiest men in the country, and President of the railroad. The boy had come to see if he could obtain a situation on the road. He said that he was an orphan—his mother had been dead only two months, and he was now a homeless wanderer. But the lad was too small for the filling of any place within the Quaker's gift, and he was forced to deny him. Still he liked the looks of the boy, and said to him:—

"You may stop in my house tonight, and tomorrow I will give the names of two or three good men of Philadelphia, to whom you may apply with assurance of kind reception at least. I am sorry that I have no employment for you."

Later in the evening the old Quaker went the rounds of his spacious mansion, lantern in hand, as was his custom, to see that all was safe, before retiring for the night. As he passed the door of the little chamber where the poor, wandering orphan had been placed to sleep, he heard a voice. He stopped and listened, and distinguished the tones of a simple, earnest prayer. He bent his ear nearer, and heard these words from the boy's lips:—

"Oh, good Father in Heaven! help me to help myself. Watch over me as I watch over my own conduct, and care for me as my deeds merit! Bless the good man in whose house I am sheltered for the night, and spare him long, that he may continue sharing his bounty to the suffering ones. Amen."

And the Quaker responded another amen as he moved on; and as he went, he meditated. The boy has a true idea of the duties of life. I verily think that the lad will be a treasure to his employer, he concluded.

When the morning came, the old Quaker changed his mind concerning his answer to the boy's application.

"Who taught you to pray?" inquired Friend L.

"My mother, sir," was the soft reply. And the rich brown eyes grew moist.

"And you will not forget your mother's counsels?"

"I cannot, for I know that my success in life is dependent upon them."

"My boy, you may stay here in my house, and very soon I will take you to my office."

Friend L. lived to see the poor boy he had adopted rise step by step until he finally assumed the responsible office which the failing guardian could no longer hold. And today there is no man more honored and respected by his friends, and none more feared by gamblers and speculators in irresponsible stock, than is the once poor wanderer—now president of the best managed and most productive railway in the United States.

Perseverance

ONE of the corporations of this city being in want of a boy in their mill, a piece of paper was tacked on one of the posts in a prominent place, so that the boys could see it as they passed. The paper read, "Boy wanted. Call at the office tomorrow morning." At the time indicated, a host of boys were waiting at the gate. All were admitted. But the overseer was a little perplexed as to the best way of choosing one from so many; and said he, "Boys, I only want one, and here are a great many; how shall I choose?" After thinking a moment, he invited them all into the yard, and driving a nail into one of the large trees, and taking a short stick, told them that the boy who could hit the nail with the stick, standing a little distance from the tree, should have the place. The boys all tried hard, and, after three trials each, signally failed to hit the nail. The boys were told to come again the next morning; and this time, when the gate was opened, there was but one boy, who, after being admitted, picked up the stick, and throwing at the nail, struck it every time.

"How is this?" said the overseer. "What have you been doing?" And the boy, looking up with tears in his eyes, said, "You see, sir, I am a poor boy. I have no father, sir; and I thought I should like to get the place, and so help my mother all I can; and, after going home yesterday, I drove a nail into the barn, and I have been trying to hit it ever since; and I have come down this morning to try again."

The boy was admitted to the place. Many years have passed since then, and now that boy is a prosperous and a wealthy man; and at the time of the burning of the Pemberton Mills, he was the first to step forward with a gift of a thousand dollars to relieve the sufferers. His success came by his perseverance.

Perseverance in any line is essential to success and prosperity.

Nothing To Do

IN another home the parents sadly neglected their only son. He was a very handsome, intelligent boy and finished school early. Now that he was through high school, and the parents refused to let him go on to college, he stood with diploma in hand wondering what to do.

For some time he tried to find a job, but he was told he was too young. No studying, no work, no companionship at home and no good books to read. What should he do, was the big question. Gradually he began to chum with other idle boys of the streets and before long got into trouble.

The proverb, "An idle brain is the devil's workshop" expresses a real truth.

Instead of the parents coming to the boy's rescue after the first offense, and providing something for him to do so he could redeem himself, he was ridiculed and mocked and shamed. He saw his wrong and tried to go straight; yet his past was constantly held before him. He finally became discouraged and said, "What's the use of staying home and being good. I am not appreciated anyhow."

No kindly adviser stepped into the breach. As a result, the boy went out again with the gang and was caught in an unlawful act. The rest of the fellows fled while this boy tried to break away from the grip of a policeman. In the struggle he unfortunately killed the officer. Well, we all know what faced him then.

A good little grandmother, who often visited the prison and provided the prisoners with wholesome reading matter, was sitting in the lobby as the young man was brought from the main office and was led down the hall by strong, stern officers. As the key was turned in the door, the young man turned his head and looked back to the entrance once more. Without words, his bewildered face said goodbye to the freedom outside. The little lady got a good view of his pale, terror-stricken face as he took that longing look toward the door and she was almost overcome with grief as she saw him disappear behind those iron doors. She wept bitterly as she went home, and she resolved to help that boy in some way and make his stay behind the bars a little less bitter. The next day she visited the institution and asked permission to see this young prisoner. The officer said: "You are in too great a hurry, grandma; he has been here only about twenty-four hours. You had better wait a few days." But she pleaded, "Good sir! I am sure these twenty-four hours have seemed as twenty-four days to the young man. I feel he needs comfort right now."

"What do you wish to do for him?" questioned the officer.

"I am going to give him this Bible to read and this little picture of the Good Shepherd to put on his bare walls. And I have baked a few cookies for him. Here, eat one so you will know they are all right."

"Yum! Yum! They are all right. He has not eaten a bite since he came here; so he may be plenty glad to get them. I will send the things over. You may go and see him."

"Thank you kindly," she answered, as she hurried over to the guard who unlocked the door for her.

Her visit, love and interest indeed proved a blessing to the bewildered boy. From week to week he looked forward to her motherly visits.

"Had my folks talked to me like you do, I would not be here," he told her one day.

After a time she noticed the boy was giving his heart to

God and one night he composed these lines:

I *lay upon my prison bed*
Pillow damp with tears I shed;
With aching heart and in despair
I cried, 'My God! There's none who care!'

" '*Twas then I heard a gentle voice,*
Which made my weary heart rejoice,
'*Oh, yes,' she said, 'God's only Son*
Has cared for you since day begun.

" '*He'll give you grace each trial to bear,*
If you appeal to Him in prayer.'
I prayed and prayed far in the night
And praying through I saw the light.

"*So now I'm happy every day,*
Happy to serve in a humble way
A Saviour born in a lowly place,
Born to die for the human race.

"*And if I in my feeble way,*
Can point to Him one who has gone astray,
I'll feel that I've not lived in vain,
Although I've done some deeds of shame.

"*To Grandma dear I give all praise,*
She led me to the Throne of Grace.
Daily now I sing His praise
Because she filled a mother's place."

"Always Be Honest"

SOME years ago a father who had lost his companion lived in the slums of one of our large cities. With him lived his little son, whom people nicknamed "Freckles." Daily this man tried to do both a father's and a mother's duty in building into his boy's heart a faith in eternal things. They lived in very meager quarters, and there was not a square foot of grass on which, or a tree under which, the child could play.

Usually Freckles had to stay home and amuse himself while his father was away working here and there at odd jobs. But one day his father took him along. As they were passing a pretty home with a spacious lawn where grew shrubs, trees, flowers and green grass, the little boy tried to pull away from his father's hand, "What is wrong, Son?" he asked.

"I want to go on that nice green grass and play until you come back, Father," he said.

"Those people will not let you play on that lawn, Son. That is their yard. They keep it very nice, don't they?" he explained to the little boy.

Freckles sighed and as they walked on, he kept looking back. The man felt keenly the lack of the temporal blessings for which the boy longed.

Upon returning to their dingy, slum home, Freckles asked, "Daddy, why can't we have some grass and flowers and trees where Johnny, Mac, and I sometimes play?"

Freckles' father was a faithful reader of the Holy Scriptures. He sat down in his chair and told the lad about the beautiful things he would be able to enjoy in the better world to come if he would be a good boy. In describing that eternal home, he said, "Listen, Sonny, when we get to that better land, we also will have a beautiful home. There we will have all kinds of lovely flowers, trees, and green grass for you to enjoy."

"Will the birds sit in our trees and sing for us, too? Will Jesus let me have a little doggie to play with?" he asked. "And will there also be a nice Shetland pony for me?"

"Yes," came the assuring answer. "I am sure Jesus will give you all the lovely things you need to be completely happy. Perhaps He will even have a nice Shetland pony for you and a fine swing in one of the trees."

Freckles never grew weary of hearing of this beautiful home. One night his father returned late. He had had a hard, long day. But little Freckles crawled up into his daddy's lap as usual and pleaded, "Daddy, please tell me again about heaven. When can we go there? How much does it cost to go there? I will go and sell some papers so that we can get the money quickly. May I, Daddy?"

Thus came the questions, one after another. The father pressed his little boy to his heart as he began, "No, my Son, you are too young to sell papers. You can help me later, but not now. If you will be a good boy and always be honest and do right, then you will someday be able to go to that beautiful home, and you will not have to pay your fare."

The boy listened very attentively, and all the while other questions arose in his anxious little heart. His father always stressed the thought that only right living would give him a home in heaven. The child was deeply impressed by what he heard.

One evening the father came home very, very tired. Not able to eat supper, he lay down on his hard bed and sighed.

"Don't you feel good, Daddy? I will rub your feet. I

know they are tired," said Freckles as he tried to rub his father's aching feet. Then he lay down beside him and soon was sound asleep.

But the man was ill. The next day he told Freckles to call the neighbor. He was now almost too ill to speak. But when the neighbor arrived, the father said, "I am worried about my little boy. If something should happen to me, would you please take care of him? He is a good boy. He will help you when he has a few more months on him. Please, will you do that for me?" But the neighbor made no promise, for she too was poor.

The sick man's fever rose rapidly. He pressed his little boy to his heart, and admonished him once more, "Dear Son, I may have to leave you, but God will always be near you. He will care for you if you will talk to Him often in prayer and always be honest. Never take anything that does not belong to you, Son. Someday you and mother and I will meet in that beautiful home which I have told you about."

With these words he fell asleep. Before morning he became delirious, and four days later the world looked very dark to little Freckles. The house seemed dreadfully empty; but it was home, and he hoped to continue there. However, this was not to be, for shortly after he had suffered his greatest loss; he was put on the street with his few belongings. Freckles could think of only one thing, and that was to find a corner where he might sell newspapers. At last he located a small nook between two buildings. He packed his few things there, then went to look for a newsboy. Finally he spied one. He ran over and gathered from him some information regarding his future work. As soon as he could get some papers he, too, stood at the street corner calling out, "Newspaper! Buy a newspaper, please."

The days were long and lonely. He hardly sold enough

to supply himself with food.

One day a little dog came sniffing along. He looked starved and homeless. Freckles talked to him and even gave him some of the dry bread he had in his pocket. Soon the nervous creature sat down and leaned against his new friend's legs. This pleased the boy very much.

When evening came, Freckles started for the little spot he now called home. The dog followed and crawled in with him. The two became fast friends. They slept together and were seen together day after day. Freckles shared his meager meals with this his only friend, who helped to keep him warm at night.

One day, when Freckles was standing at his usual place and calling out his papers, a well-dressed lady dropped her purse as she stepped into her beautiful, shiny car and drove away. Freckles picked it up and looked into it. There he saw many shiny dollars. Would he take some?

"Oh, no," he said to himself. "They are not mine. I will run after the car. Perhaps I can catch up with it at the stoplight at the end of the block."

Off he went, with his little dog right at his heels. He ran up to the car, waving the purse at the lady. "Oh, thank you!" she said, and tossed him a tip.

The lady was greatly pleased with the little newsboy's honesty. She felt that she ought to do something for him. After much meditation, she was impressed to adopt him if she could do so. She began procedures at once.

A number of weeks later, she drove up to the corner where stood the dirty, weary, freckle-faced newsboy. She called him to her car and asked to buy some papers. He had about a dozen under his arm. She bought them all. Freckles was happily surprised.

"Come, get into my car. I want to give you a ride. You have no papers to sell now," the lady suggested.

Freckles hesitated a bit as he looked at her beautiful

clothes and lovely car. Then he said, "Thank you, Madam, but I am only a newsboy. I do not have nice clothes. Besides, I have a little partner. I call him Nip, and myself I call Tuck, because with us it is nip and tuck to make a living." He continued with a smile, "He goes with me
wherever I go. He is the only friend I have."

"I am glad you have a friend. Let Nip come in too," she replied.

Freckles and Nip entered and settled down as the lady drove off. Soon they were out of the busy business district and were winding around in an attractive residential section. Freckles was wishing his father could be enjoying the ride with him, seeing the pretty houses and clean streets. Suddenly they were driving up a long hill. When they reached the top, they drove into a beautiful yard. As they neared the house he saw a swing in a tree, and beside the tree stood a Shetland pony.

The car stopped, and the lady opened the door. "Step out, Son, and enjoy yourself! This is your home. That Shetland pony will be yours, and Nip may stay too," she said.

Freckles looked around nervously and excitedly; then taking hold of the lady's hand and looking into her face, he asked, "Is this heaven? If it is, please take me to my father."

Tears filled her eyes, as she answered the boy's question. "I will do my best to make this a little heaven for you until Jesus comes to take us all to His great heaven. I hope that when we shall enter into that beautiful place, you will see your father and mother again. Jesus will be there too. Won't that be wonderful?"

"But - - but, my father told me that heaven was a beautiful place like this; and that - - that - - . Well, it is just like he told me. Please tell me, is this heaven?" he continued.

The kind woman took the lad into the house, washed him, and put new clothes on him. Then she said, "Freckles, my boy, you do not have to go back to selling papers. I am going to adopt you, and you will be my little boy."

"Oh! You talk just like my daddy did. How did you know that I prayed for a home? I was very lonesome after my father died," said Freckles.

"Shall I tell you how I knew?" she asked.

Freckles looked rather surprised while he listened to his new mother as she read, *"The eyes of the Lord are upon the righteous, and his ears are open unto their cry."* Ps. 34:15. *"The righteous cry, and the Lord heareth, and delivereth them out of all their troubles."* Ps. 34:17. Then she added, "God heard your cries; and because you were honest, I was impressed to bring you home and adopt you as my boy."

The Lord heard the earnest prayers of Freckles and answered them by placing him in a beautiful home of the kind woman.